Return to Me

Deborah Pierson Dill

Return to Me

Contact Information: titleadmin@pelicanbookgroup.com

Cover Art by *Nicola Martinez*

White Rose Publishing, a division of Pelican Ventures, LLC
www.whiterosepublishing.com PO Box 1738 *Aztec, NM * 87410

White Rose Publishing Circle and Rosebud logo is a trademark of Pelican Ventures, LLC

Publishing History
First White Rose Edition, 2011
Print Edition ISBN 978-1-61116-074-1
Electronic Edition ISBN 978-1-61116-075-8
Published in the United States of America

Books by Deborah Pierson Dill

Perfect Shelter
Return to Me
Moving On

Dedication

To the Lord, who placed the heart's desire within me.
And to the family who consistently encouraged me to
pursue it.

1

The buzzards circling overhead should have been her first clue.

Actually, her stupid car's air conditioner—busted again on this, the eleventh day in a row of triple digit heat index—should have been her *first* clue. But the buzzards circling overhead, waiting for something to drop dead from heat stroke, should have been the clearest clue that this day would soon go completely down in flames.

Audrey Rhodes clutched her purse, raising it to her chest like a shield, and stood blinking, frozen despite the heat in the middle of the Prickly Pear Café, face to face with the boy who had thoroughly broken her heart ten years ago. Since that time she had referred to him only as, "what's-his-name." But not because she couldn't remember his real name. Try as she might, she would never forget him.

The years hadn't changed him, except to add a definitive manliness to his looks and generally improve on what Audrey already considered perfection. He had the same head full of wavy, dark blond hair; the same green eyes that hinted how he could show a girl the time of her life; the same dimpled, easy smile; the same lean, muscular build.

Now he stood three feet away, directing that smile at her, like he just knew he could still make her toes curl if she'd let him. Her heart began to skip and palpitate, and her stomach went all twisty inside like it hadn't done since she'd been a girl. But even as every nerve screamed for her to cross the distance between them and slap him, she felt a slow smile emerge.

Then he opened his mouth to speak.

"Hi, Audrey. Remember me? Brent Thomason?"

That did it!

Every shred of sentimentality vanished. Audrey turned and slapped a twenty-dollar bill down, the sound of her palm hitting the counter underscoring the hush that had fallen all around. The whispering voices of former classmates bringing lunch companions up to speed on the back-story may have been real or imagined. But either way, in the span of about twenty seconds, he managed to make her a public spectacle yet again.

Audrey snatched her change from the confused looking teenaged girl behind the counter and grabbed the sack full of burgers she'd come for. Then she turned around to face him again.

How dare he! How could she have, even for one second, forgotten the insensitivity, the callousness of this…this…boy? The audacity of him, reintroducing himself like that! As if what had gone on between them had been so inconsequential that she might not even remember him.

"Brent." She ground out his name and pushed past him coldly.

"Audrey, wait."

She gritted her teeth and turned back to see him throw his check and a few bills on the counter, then thrust his hand out impatiently for his change while the poor cashier rang him up as fast as she could. She knew the value of a dollar as well as anyone, but that bit of action only served to irritate her further. Let him chase her if he wanted to talk.

"Audrey, wait!"

She'd made it halfway across the sizzling asphalt parking lot before she heard him call. She yanked the car door open and tossed her purse and the burgers across to the passenger seat as he caught up.

"Audrey..." He sounded incredulous. Like he couldn't believe she wouldn't weep for joy and throw herself into his arms at this chance encounter. "That's it?"

Audrey stopped and turned to face him. Was that actually confusion registered on his face? "Well, Brent, let's see. I could say how good it is to see you. But, you know, it's really not. I guess I could ask how you've been. Except that I don't care. What else is there?"

"Well, there's 'hello,' for one. Or, 'what brings you back to town?' And I get the distinct impression that maybe you *do* care a little."

What right did he have to be so contentious? After the way he'd treated her...

Audrey narrowed her eyes and glared at him for a brief moment, then got into the car and slammed the door, remembering too late that the action wouldn't put an end to their conversation because she'd left the windows down.

"Come on, Audrey–"

"OK, how about this? You never called."

He gave his head a perplexed shake. "What?"

"I believe your exact words were, 'I'll call you tomorrow. *I promise.*'"

Brent blinked at her. Clearly, this wasn't the line of conversation he'd hoped for.

"Audrey, I'm sorry...I just didn't–"

"You know what? Never mind. I really don't want to hear your pretend apology. It's about ten years too late, anyway."

Brent placed both his hands on the car door, preventing her from putting up the window. But she didn't even try. Earlier she'd nearly branded herself with the seatbelt buckle. The car door had to burn like the handle of a hot iron skillet. A silent minute ticked by as she waited for him to move.

"Sure is hot out today," he said at last, as a little bead of sweat trickled down the side of his face.

Audrey froze, her hand poised to turn the key in the ignition and steer the car away, not bothering to care if she ran over his foot in the process. Then she felt it; the smile that emerged slowly, without her consent. She tried to subdue it. It started somewhere inside, in response to what, she couldn't even say. Anger boiled right up to the surface when she looked at him. Still, there he stood with that unpretentious, irresistible smile, thoroughly honest about and unapologetic for the kind of guy he was. In her wildest dreams she never thought she could feel glad to see him again. But some part of her did.

She sighed. "Yes, it is." Then she turned the key, started the car, and put it in gear.

"Maybe I'll see you around?" He sounded hopeful.

Audrey shook her head. "Not if I can help it."

⁂

Brent stood in the middle of the parking lot watching Audrey's retreating car as the heat radiating from the asphalt all but singed the hair off his arms. She was mad at him. Livid might more adequately describe it. All because he hadn't called?

He couldn't deny his guilt. Ten years ago he *had* promised to call. In fact, he very clearly remembered promising her much more than that. If she was only mad because he hadn't called...well his guilt extended far beyond that, and he knew better than to think her anger only extended to that particular injury.

Brent pushed a hand through his hair and rubbed the back of his neck. The way he'd treated her shamed him. He had used her, then cast her off like...what? He couldn't think of anything for which he would show so little regard now. And the heat made it nearly impossible to think straight about anything. And those buzzards circling overhead couldn't possibly be a good sign.

The air conditioning in his new pickup provided little relief this afternoon, but he adjusted the vents anyway, trying to direct as much cool air as possible his way. He could remember some hot summers here. But he didn't remember a time when so many fields had lain dead and ruined from heat and drought. Hundreds of acres had suffered the ravages of wildfires, leaving entire pastures and long stretches of right of way along the highway charred black. He couldn't remember the summers taking such a toll on the environment. But he had a different perspective now.

On the drive back here from College Station, he passed a few farms with irrigation systems running. But even so, their crops were withering. Livestock herds in fields along the way looked smaller than they should, and what cattle and goats did graze appeared too lean as they foraged for whatever sustenance they could gather from dying land. And that wasn't the only problem, or even the biggest. Every stock tank he noticed had been nearly dry if not completely so. This could be a devastating summer.

Brent adjusted the air vents again in a vain attempt to direct more cold air his way, and slowed to a stop for the first of two major intersections in town. He glanced around at the strangely foreign, yet familiar surroundings. A new convenience store stood proudly on one corner, just across from an old one that sagged, abandoned like so many other buildings that, to his knowledge, hadn't been occupied in decades. No, not much had changed. Except his perspective.

Blithe Settlement was a hot, central Texas town– not quite far enough south to be considered part of the hill country, not far enough east to completely escape the West Texas dust. Right in the middle, it sat, where two or three terrains blended on their way to becoming something else. Three hours or more away from every major city in the state. The middle of nowhere.

Still, it felt good to be home.

He turned off the highway and into the parking lot of an unassuming brown brick building. It was flanked by a caliche parking lot and an array of animal pens and stalls which filled the space between the building and a good sized pole barn. The Rhodes Veterinary Clinic.

His one o'clock appointment with Lyndon Rhodes awaited him.

Audrey was pretty mad now. Brent could only pity the poor soul chosen to give her the news that he'd come home to stay, and would most likely be working for her father.

☙❧

Audrey dropped her purse and the sack of burgers on her desk, then turned the dial of the oscillating fan on top of the filing cabinet as high as it would go. She sank into the chair and eyed the sack of burgers, not really hungry anymore. Then she twisted her hair and tried to hold it up off her neck for a moment.

She opened the top desk drawer and shuffled through it looking for a hair clip. There had to be one somewhere. An irritated grumble slipped from her throat as she pushed the contents of the drawer around. Last time she'd opened this drawer there had been two clips right there. But now they were gone. It figured.

What's the point? She let her thick hair fall back down.

Cooling off wouldn't make her feel any better now. It was a shame, too, because Audrey had just recently begun to feel the pieces of her life falling back into place again, like things had finally taken a turn for the better.

Unfortunately, it only took the sight of Brent Thomason to drag her right back down again. The memory of how stupid and weak she was, and probably always would be, nearly crushed the notion that she would ever have a reasonable amount of control over anything.

She couldn't blame Brent, really. She'd known what kind of boy he was all those years ago. Being mad at him for how he treated her was like getting mad at your cat after it caught and killed your pet hamster when you'd been the one who left the cage open.

Truthfully, she was angrier for succumbing to the stupid teenage fantasy that *she* would somehow be different to him–that her love could change him. Brent had only done what he always did. Unfortunately, her tragic taste in men had begun with him and continued on, just as tragically, once he'd gone. Audrey sighed and laid her head on the cool veneer surface of her desk.

"What happened to you?"

Audrey turned her head without raising it, getting a sideways view of Carlene Fletcher, who leaned against her office doorjamb, arms folded across her chest. Carlene came to dig around in the bag on Audrey's desk, looking for her hamburger.

"I ran into Brent Thomason at the Prickly Pear just now," Audrey said.

"Old what's-his-name? What's he doin' back in town?"

"I don't know."

Carlene stopped digging and looked up at Audrey, a slow smile spreading across her face. Then she pulled a burger out of the sack, opened it, and began picking at it.

"Brent Thomason..." Carlene's tone changed when she said his name. Suddenly she sounded all dreamy and contemplative.

Audrey finally raised her head.

"What do you mean, you don't know?" Carlene made it back to the present. She perched on the corner of Audrey's desk, one leg crossed over the other with a black, strappy sling back dangling from her toes. "Where's he been? What's he been up to? How's he doing?"

Audrey shrugged and reached for her own burger.

"Did you talk to him at all?"

"Not any more than I had to."

Carlene just looked at her as if she'd gone completely stupid. Then realization lit her face. "Oh, that's right," she drawled. "You were the last in the Brent Thomason Trail of Tears. I guess *that* explains the condition of this burger."

Should she smile at the melodrama or cringe at the tactless exaggeration? Audrey didn't know. Finally she nodded. She had been the very last. Brent had left town the next day. Of course, with Brent one could never tell, there could have been two or three more that night. That's the way he worked. But she'd probably been the very last girl between the ages of seventeen and twenty-one in the town of Blithe Settlement to give in to his charm.

Carlene had given in a lot sooner and more than once if the rumors were true. Audrey had been so jealous. And maybe it was jealousy that made her so certain that Carlene was not the kind of girl she should extend friendship to.

Audrey bit her bottom lip, shame stinging at the memory of her youthful arrogance. They hadn't been friends in high school. Most of their senior year they'd been competitors for the affection of one what's-his-name, even though she and her Sunday school morality didn't stand a chance when pitted against a girl like Carlene Fletcher. And Carlene probably had no idea about Audrey's feelings for Brent.

Carlene had always tried to be too sophisticated for a little town like this. Who knew where her inspiration came from? It probably had something to do with the stack of *Cosmopolitan* magazines she kept piled in one corner of her office. Although she did a better job of it now than she had ten years ago, she still never quite managed to pull it off.

Audrey stifled a snort and looked down at her burger. *Or maybe she does. How would I know?*

She cast a glance where Carlene sat in a skirt that was a little too short and a little too tight; with her dark hair piled up on top of her head just a few tendrils falling down for effect; with her eyebrows tweezed pencil thin, smoky eye makeup, and red lipstick. Audrey's gaze traveled down Carlene's leg to the sparkly, red pedicured toes which toyed precariously with her dangling shoe. Suddenly she could remember with absolute clarity why they had never been friendly in school.

But then they'd graduated, old points of contention fading as they became fully immersed in the world of jobs, bills, and independence. Eventually both had ended up working at the real estate office; Carlene as an agent, Audrey typing, filing, making coffee, sweeping crickets off the front porch in the mornings, and other duties as assigned. Despite their former opposition, they had gotten to know each other and had become friends.

*Still...*Audrey sighed. A bit of the old animosity reared up at the thought that what's-his-name was back in town.

"So what *did* you say to him?" Carlene's voice brought Audrey back to the present.

"I pointed out the fact that he never called."

Silence.

"What?" Carlene asked, incredulously. Then she laughed. "And what did he say to that?"

"I think he started to apologize. Then I told him I didn't really care, and I got in my car and drove off."

Carlene stared at her.

"I thought about running over his foot."

Carlene laughed again. "His foot? If I was mad enough to run over some part of Brent Thomason, it wouldn't be his foot."

ॐॐ

"Dadgummit, Gertie!" Audrey blew out a frustrated growl.

As if this day hadn't been irritating enough already. Now she had to contend with this. And there wasn't even anyone she could call to complain to. No one actually claimed Gertie, but everybody knew her name. She wore a collar and a bell, was generally indifferent to humans, and on any given day, could be found relaxing on the hood of Audrey's car. It made no difference where she parked–shade, sun, rain, hail.

It wouldn't have been so bad had Gertie been a cat. A dog would have been a bit more troublesome, but still acceptable under the circumstances. No such luck. Gertie was a solid black Pygmy goat with one bright white patch right between her horns. And there she sat this blistering Friday afternoon, atop the car hood, front hooves tucked neatly underneath her, chewing cud.

Audrey grabbed for one of the goat's horns, a maneuver which was usually sure to bring her to her feet. But today, she was met with a warning tap from the goat's horns and a half-hearted bleat. A second tactic, pushing the animal from behind, worked. Gertie finally budged and lumbered down, leaving one or two new dents and scratches in her cloven-hoofed wake.

The car felt like an oven when Audrey slid inside. She turned the key in the ignition and tested the temperature of the steering wheel with the tips of her fingers, wanting nothing more than to go home, turn her meager window units as high and cool as they would go, and lay on her couch watching television and eating ice cream until she fell asleep. But she'd promised her parents she'd come for dinner tonight. And as much as she wanted to, she couldn't back out.

Her relationship with her folks had been turbulent the past several years. Since she'd broken up with Bobby, things had evened out some. But not enough that she felt like she could cancel dinner plans without them bringing their "tough love" to her house to find out what the problem was now; to make sure she wasn't falling back into the same trap that had ensnared her before. So she turned the car in the direction of their house, smiling a little at the ultimate sense of comfort and belonging that eased frustration as it came into view.

Home.

A horse's whinny drifted on the breeze from the clinic as she stepped out of the car, the sound reminding her of the childhood spent here, safe, secure, happy. So many times she should have run back to this security. Her parents had begged her to when they realized the violent turn her life with Bobby had taken. How much sooner might she have sorted out the whole mess if she'd just come back when she'd had the chance?

"Hey, Mom." Audrey called a greeting from the utility room entrance before pausing briefly in the guest powder room to rinse her face and wash her hands. Then she joined her mother in the kitchen.

"Hi, baby. Would you mind setting the table?"

"You'll never guess who I ran into today." Audrey picked up a stack of her mother's best china—*her best china*. It gave her a little pause, but she took it to the dining room table without a word. Four place settings. Someone else was coming to dinner. Some kind of weird bad feeling sunk itself into her gut.

"Oh? Who?" Paula Rhodes was busy with a pot on the stove.

Audrey's heart sank and she hung her head. Her mom sounded way too nonchalant. "Brent Thomason. Remember him?"

"Mm-hm."

Audrey finished setting the plates and returned to the kitchen. "OK, what do you know about it?" But the pieces had already fallen together.

Somewhere in the recesses of her mind she vaguely recalled that Brent had left to pursue a career in veterinary medicine at Texas A&M. When Audrey combined that bit of circumstantial evidence with the fact that her father was looking to hire a new vet, the situation began to look very grim.

"Audrey." Her mom tapped a spoon on the side of a pot and then replaced the lid. "I don't recall what exactly happened between the two of you. I know you were heart broken when he left. But that was years ago. You were a girl. Surely it wasn't that bad. And you two were such good friends when you were children."

Audrey hardly heard a word her mother said. Her mind latched greedily onto the idea that Brent had never been much of a student. It was quite possible–probable, in fact–that he'd never finished school, and his appearance in town today was nothing more than a bizarre coincidence.

13

"Whatever it was," her mother was saying when Audrey's mind drifted back to their conversation, "try to forget about it for now. Be nice to him at dinner. Your father would like him to take the job."

The doorbell rang before Audrey could respond. Her mom whipped off her apron, smoothed her hair, and headed for the front door. Audrey could already hear her dad's voice welcoming what's-his-name into their home.

Audrey stopped in the dining room, aware that any second the three of them would turn the corner out of the foyer and there she'd be, in plain view. They'd be able to see this emotion–what was it? shame? humiliation?–all over her.

She took a deep breath, determined to cover it. At least she had a few seconds to prepare, unlike earlier at the Prickly Pear when she almost ran right into him.

She could do this. A deep breath in, then out, nearly convinced her. She could suffer through dinner. Then she wouldn't have to see him again, other than here and there around town. Certainly she wouldn't have to have another conversation with him. Fortunately, there was no chance of her getting suckered by him a second time. She'd learned the hard way what he was all about. She was older, wiser, and she knew better now. A lot better.

"...and I'm sure you remember my daughter, Audrey," her dad said as they came into the dining room.

"How could I forget Audrey?" Brent said, charm oozing.

And just what was *that* supposed to mean?

Audrey raised her narrowed eyes to meet his and saw the same expression she'd always remembered on him. There was his grin; his wide, maddeningly soft mouth, perfect teeth, beautifully defined jaw. There were his eyes; green, mischievous, mocking her. But there seemed to be an earnestness about his expression she didn't remember ever seeing before. Then, of course, there was the rest of him; strong, broad shoulders, straight lines, confident stance.

"I meant to tell you this when I ran into you earlier." Brent's voice sounded smooth, almost honest. "It's real good to see you again."

He didn't touch her. But Audrey could tell he wanted to reach out and take her hand or something. Her knees nearly buckled at the thought.

Nope. No way was Brent Thomason going to get to her again.

2

Somehow Audrey made it through dinner without screaming or choking. She tried to listen politely as her father and Brent discussed the terms of Brent's possible employment, the weather, and the Dallas Cowboys. But her mind reeled back to an oppressively hot August night ten years ago.

Brent had finally turned his attention and his charm to her. She wasn't much of a challenge, but he pursued her relentlessly, anyway, knowing she had a crush on him, and using that knowledge to his advantage.

"I don't know why it's taken me so long to realize how much you mean to me." He brushed her long, blonde hair back off of her shoulder and kissed her cheek, sending a flood of tingles down her spine, the sensation all new and wonderful. He drew her down to sit beside him on the battered, stained couch in the mobile home where he lived with his mother. Then he wrapped an arm around her shoulders and leaned in to place a few more breathy little kisses on her cheek, near her ear, trailing down onto her neck.

"Brent, don't." She resisted his advance, pressing him away. "What if your Mom comes home?"

He grinned and shook his head. "She won't."

Then he kissed her with lips so soft and warm she melted completely, unable to believe that the boy she loved finally noticed her as something more than a friend. When his fingers undid the top button of her blouse, every muscle tensed. She reached for his hands to stop him.

"Brent, no–"

"You're so beautiful." He kissed her again.

"We shouldn't–"

"How could I have not seen it before?" He pressed her down onto her back.

"But, I think–"

"I really think you might just be the one for me." He leaned over, stroking her hair and gazing into her eyes, expertly nestling between her thighs in a way that disturbed and thrilled her all at the same time. "I think I love you, Audrey."

Her breath caught in her chest. "You love me?"

He nodded. "How could I not?"

An ecstatic smile warmed her, and she wound her arms around his neck as he kissed her again, deeply. The way a man kisses the woman he loves.

When he started on her buttons again she didn't stop him. Part of her wanted to. She didn't want her first time to be here, in this dingy mobile home on this nasty sofa. And she had no intention of letting things go that far. But she longed for him to love her. And if letting him go just a little farther secured that love then what could be the harm? He needed her.

But things had gone much too far.

A half hour later as Audrey sat in his truck listening to the engine idle, reality hit hard. Everything he had done and said had been to this precise end.

"I'll call you tomorrow." He didn't kiss her. He wouldn't even look at her for more than a fleeting second or two.

Her self-respect shattered. But he must have seen the skepticism alongside the tears in her eyes. He raised one hand to brush her hair behind her ear. Then he pulled her against him.

"I promise," he whispered in her ear.

Audrey blinked away the present sting of tears and looked down at her empty dinner plate. She so wanted to believe him. Maybe it was something in the words, *I promise,* or perhaps the way he'd said them. But in that moment, she convinced herself that he would call, and they'd have a bright future. Together.

All the rationalizations still echoed in her mind. *Surely he isn't this sincere with the other girls. How could he be? I'm the one who really loves him. That has to mean something. He couldn't not respond to that, could he?*

The unfortunate truth was, however, that he lied. He never called. After a few days she gathered enough courage to ask around about him. Then she learned the truth about his promises. He'd known when he made that promise he wouldn't be around to keep it. His destination was College Station and Texas A&M University, where his goal would be, no doubt, to leave another string of broken hearts in another region of Texas.

Knowing how many girls Brent Thomason had made such promises to would be impossible. He'd probably lied to all of them. *I promise* meant nothing special to him. But her greatest fear remained: That somewhere there lived a girl he'd been sincere with, a girl he loved. And it wasn't her. *She* had meant nothing special to him.

"I promise," her dad was saying as her mind shifted back to the present situation, "you won't regret your decision to come home."

Brent nodded and glanced at her. "It'll probably be one of the few decisions I haven't regretted."

As the two men rose from the table to continue their conversation in the comfort of the living room, the women rose to clear the dishes. She couldn't even look at her mother. Earlier her mom said she didn't remember what had caused the conflict between her and Brent. But sooner or later it would come back to her. Rumors had flown.

Audrey clearly remembered the points and glances from all of Brent's buddies in the weeks that followed the evening she'd spent with him. No one ever said anything to her, and eventually, it seemed, all was forgotten as everyone grew up and moved on. But her mother must have heard about it from someone, or overheard it in the conversation of another.

It had always been a foregone conclusion that whichever girl Brent took out on Saturday night would be his newest source of bragging rights on Monday morning. And she had no idea why she thought the outcome would be any different for her. If she correctly remembered her naiveté, it had been something along the lines of her love changing him. Their friendship had begun in second grade. He couldn't possibly think of her as just another conquest.

She smiled regretfully at the thought, pushed open the back screen door, and stepped out onto the patio. The sun had not yet begun to set, but an evening breeze cooled the air around her. She breathed deeply.

That's what she used to think. The love of a good woman could reform any man. She used to think it was as simple as that. It had been an idea she willingly compromised almost every principle to believe in.

There is a love that can reform any man.

The thought came to her on the warm evening breeze as she sat down and propped her feet up, squeezing her eyes shut to force it away. She didn't want to deal with the things the still small voice had been whispering lately. She had strayed so far from that way, and done so when she clearly knew better, had been raised knowing better.

No. She shook her head to clear it. She would continue, secure in her salvation and grateful for it but not hoping or wishing for anything more.

The screen door creaked behind her. Then came heavy footsteps on the concrete patio.

"I came to say thanks for dinner."

She closed her eyes and took another deep, fortifying breath at the warm, masculine sound of his voice. "It wasn't my idea."

"Well, thanks, anyway." Brent sat in the wrought iron chair next to hers and took a deep breath of his own. "I guess it's gonna cool off pretty nice."

Audrey nodded, letting her gaze latch onto the lithe, gray form of Dad's cat as it scaled the backyard fence.

"I think it'll be good to be back home." He sounded confident despite Audrey's cold shoulder. "There's only so much of a big town like College Station that a boy like me can take. It's a different world there, everyone rushing around, no time to make friends. It's hard to find people who have things in common with you."

Audrey wanted to laugh at that. She wanted to snap and say she figured there'd be plenty just like him in a place like College Station. But she kept her mouth shut.

"I guess if I'm gonna be moving back permanently

I'll need to start looking for a place to live."

"Well, good luck." She stood abruptly, snatched her half finished glass of iced tea from the table and turned to leave.

"Audrey, please wait."

This made the second time today he entreated her to wait. His voice sounded completely guileless and even a little hurt. For an instant she felt the slightest bit of remorse for her rudeness. But Brent was a con artist. A sincere plea was a trick of the trade for him.

"I know you're mad at me," he said. "I don't blame you. But can't we—"

"I'm not mad at you, Brent." It felt strange to call him by his name after so many years. "Being mad at you would be pointless. I didn't appreciate being used, then lied to. Especially by someone I *thought* was at least my friend. But it wasn't really your fault. You were just being you. I didn't *have* to say 'yes' to you. No one made me. What happened between us was my own fault."

Brent looked down at his boots.

She'd hurt his feelings, and an unexpected surge of tears filled her eyes. She swallowed, took a breath and bit back an apology.

"Audrey, I know I treated you badly. You didn't deserve it. No one did..." Brent paused and drew a deep breath. "But you...you were...we *were* friends, and I ruined that. I am truly sorry."

Audrey stood there and blinked, too stunned to respond. Too much more of this tender brand of sincerity could easily wear her down again. Already an overwhelming and unexpected desire to forgive him took hold. But she'd learned the hard way that a man's apologies usually meant nothing. She needed to remember that.

Empty words.

Audrey nodded and turned again to leave.

"I mean it, Audrey," he said as she opened the back door. "I'm sorry."

☙❧

As luck would have it, the desk clerk at the ironically named Four Star Motel didn't know Brent, and he was glad for that.

Back in school, one of the weekend desk clerks had been his buddy, Kyle Clayton. Kyle could always be counted on to make sure Brent got a room, despite the fact that the motel's policy strictly prohibited renting rooms to minors.

Not that Brent had needed motel rooms on a regular basis.

His father had run off before he was even born, and his mother wasn't around much either. As a result, Brent spent most of his life unsupervised. Usually, he just took his dates back to his home.

Brent unlocked the sturdy metal door, pushed it open and stepped into the stuffy little room. The place hadn't changed one bit. He dropped his small suitcase by the door, turned on the light, and then the air conditioner. With a heavy sigh he rubbed a hand across the back of his neck and dropped down onto the bed.

Until he actually arrived today, Brent had looked forward to coming home. Now, however, coming back didn't seem like such a great idea. Audrey's reaction alone convinced him that he might not be as well received as he'd hoped.

Audrey.

Her name had come to mind first when he heard of the job here, and not just because the clinic belonged to her father. The coldness with which she'd treated him tonight had hurt, not that he expected her to be glad to see him. But her not speaking to him made asking forgiveness difficult.

The apology he attempted tonight on the patio was completely inadequate. When he followed her outside he'd intended to do more than merely make amends for his former behavior. He wanted to tell her how much he'd changed. He wanted to tell her that he was a completely different man now, and he was not only sorry for what he'd done, but also for what he'd been.

You were just being you.

Her words from their earlier conversation had grown immense and hung heavily in the atmosphere. Haunting him with their truth.

Of all the people here, Audrey would be the one who understood the changes in him. She would understand his conversion, or so he had hoped. Brent opened the side table drawer next to him and pulled out the Gideon Bible which had probably been stashed there since the dawn of time. He ran a hand across the cover and then opened it and fanned the pages.

Audrey had never been ashamed to speak of or demonstrate her faith in God. Back in school she'd had a genuine concern for his spiritual well being. But church and religion and God had been nothing more than an arbitrary set of rules devised by some vague authority to keep everyone in line. And he'd seen it as his mission to break as many of those rules as possible. His own personal mission field, he used to say whenever Audrey brought it up.

He snapped the Bible shut and laid it on the table.

Brent had nearly flunked out of college by his sophomore year. He spent his nights at parties or sometimes with girls he didn't know. He'd consumed more alcohol than he wanted to estimate, and experimented with drugs of all kinds. He'd skipped his classes, failed assignments, and ended up on academic probation after one semester. That had turned into academic suspension the next semester.

Then he planned to take a semester or two "off," as most kids on academic suspension liked to phrase it, working enough to pay his portion of the rent and buy junk food and beer to sustain him until his next paycheck. But those couple of semesters quickly turned into a couple of years.

One evening, during a phone conversation with one of his old friends back home, he asked about Audrey. He had no clue why. The question just slipped out. And the answer...She'd hooked up with Bobby Kerr, the school bully who had grown up to be an even bigger bully, with a penchant for spending all his girlfriends' money on alcohol, then going home to slap them around while under the influence. A Kerr family tradition.

The news broke Brent's heart, and that surprised him. He'd never been one to feel much for other people. But Audrey deserved so much better. She'd been a friend to him. He had taken advantage of her gentle heart, and even he couldn't explain why.

Brent never wanted to use her that way. They'd always been friends, and he valued her friendship. In fact, if there had ever been anyone for whom he had felt true affection, it was Audrey. Still, he had employed every underhanded trick he knew to lure her back to his mother's crappy trailer. Afterwards she'd sat in his truck with tears in her eyes, finally seeing him for what he really was.

He'd never wanted to go back and undo anything so badly. And then, finding out she was with Bobby Kerr who mostly likely treated her even worse...

Maybe guilt or shame drove him out to the nearest bar that night. Or it might simply have been the familiar daily urge to numb his mind and body to his hardened heart. Whatever drove him didn't matter because he never made it past the parking lot.

He accidentally bumped shoulders with a belligerent cowboy who turned suddenly and threatened to beat him senseless. The cowboy might have done so, too, had he not been too inebriated to stand on his own two feet. A woman in the tightest, shortest skirt he'd ever seen supported him with an arm around his waist. She was half his size, and appeared to be handling her wine only slightly better.

The two turned and stumbled away. Brent shook his head and turned back to the bar trying to remember that cliché he'd always heard. Something about the grace of God.

"There, but for the grace of God, go I..."

He could have sworn he only thought about the phrase. He hadn't said anything aloud. But he heard the words coming from behind him and he spun to see a thin, gray-haired man, fixing him with a soul-piercing stare.

"There, but for the grace of God, go you," the stranger finished.

He glanced back at the cowboy who now fumbling with the key to his truck. Then he turned back to the stranger in time to see his frail form turn the corner and disappear.

Brent sighed and leaned back against the headboard. God had spoken to him through that stranger, had reached right down, taken him by the shoulders and given him a good hard shake. Had shown him the future of his present course and quietly offered another path.

The incident changed his life.

He didn't go into that bar or any bar that night, or ever again. The next Sunday he found his way to a small church about two blocks from his apartment, stayed after the service to talk to the pastor, and two weeks later he professed his newfound faith publicly to the congregation there. He hadn't had a drink since, although he'd often fought the familiar urge to drink himself silly at some setback or disappointment.

Now, for instance.

≈

"So, what do you think? Is it gonna rain today?"

Every morning someone walked into the office and asked the same question. It didn't matter that there wasn't a cloud in the sky. Speculating about the chances of rain each day had become a ritual. This morning Carlene had thrown it out there. She sounded suspiciously cheerful.

"It's never gonna rain again," Audrey grumbled.

"Of course it will." Carlene flipped the light switch on the wall just inside her office door, then shed her suit jacket and threw it over the back of a chair. "What's with the doom and gloom this morning? It wouldn't have anything to do with the fact that old what's-his-name is going to be working for your father, would it?"

Audrey sat down behind her desk and turned on the computer. Then she glanced up at Carlene, who leaned against her office doorway and examined her bright red fingernails.

"Word travels fast."

The bell on the front door rang and Audrey looked up, thankful for the distraction. Jim Carlson, their boss, came through the door.

"Morning, Audrey." He greeted her then stopped, right in the middle of the room and looked at Carlene for a long minute, a slow smile emerging. "Carlene."

"Good morning, Jim." Her tone sounded artificially indifferent, and she smiled back as she brushed past him on her way to the coffee pot behind Audrey's desk.

Jim continued past them, down the hall to his office.

Audrey spun around in her chair.

Carlene busied herself with a coffee filter, a smile still curving her lips.

"Is there something you want to talk about?" Audrey whispered.

Measuring the coffee grounds into the filter, Carlene only smiled wider. Then she picked up the pot. "I need to get some water for this."

"Carlene!"

The little bell on the front door jingled again and Audrey spun to face Brent, who stood there, looking a little ill at ease as his glance vacillated between her and Carlene. Finally he cast his gaze to the floor and removed his baseball cap.

"Good morning." He managed to glance back at

her as he folded his worn cap in half and stuffed it in his back jeans pocket. "I thought I'd get a start on looking for a place before I head back home to settle things there. I was thinking maybe you could help me out, Audrey."

"Um..." She paused to keep from stammering. "You'll need to talk to Carlene about that, Brent. I'm not a real estate agent."

"Oh." He shifted his glance to Carlene.

"Well, Brent Thomason!" Audrey could have sworn Carlene's voice dropped at least an octave. "I was wonderin' when you'd get out here to see me. Come on into my office, and we'll see what we can find. Would you like some coffee? I was just about to put some on."

"No. Thanks."

Carlene set the pot in its place and turned back to him with a hundred watt smile.

Audrey couldn't look at them as Brent followed Carlene to her office. She was asking what he'd been doing for the past ten years.

Audrey turned her chair toward the filing cabinet.

"So were you thinking of renting or are you more of a mind to buy?" Carlene asked.

"I was thinking I'd like to buy a house," Brent said as Carlene closed her office door.

A most unwelcome animosity rose with the heat that crept up Audrey's neck and into her face.

Carlene Fletcher never closed her office door when she was with a client.

Audrey launched from her chair to the filing cabinet. *Good grief!* What difference did it make if Carlene closed her door? She couldn't care less how Carlene behaved with Brent. The two could take up just as they had back in school for all she cared. They could be in there all over each other right now, and it wouldn't bother her in the least.

They may not have changed, but she had. The last thing she needed was another man who would use, manipulate, and abuse her. She could swear she still had bruises leftover from her association with Bobby Kerr.

Brent may never have shoved her into walls or over furniture, or struck her across the face with the back of his hand, but he had never been any more interested in her welfare than if he had. She could do better.

So why did the sight of him walking through the door just now reduce her insides to something resembling warm jelly? How was she to explain the lump that rose to her throat and the tears that stung at the thought of him in there alone with Carlene and all her *Cosmo* inspired wiles? What was wrong with her?

Not fifteen minutes passed before Carlene's door opened and the two emerged, both smiling. Audrey turned back to her filing.

"You sure you can't stick around a while?" Carlene said. "I already have a few places in mind that sound like what you're looking for. I could show them to you."

"No, I really need to hit the road," Brent said. "I'll be back this weekend."

"Then I'll do some checking, and next Monday morning we'll go out and have a look around."

"Thanks," Brent said, then he paused. "I guess I'll see y'all in a week, then."

Audrey didn't turn around.

3

"So, what's the story?"

Leave it to Carlene to start Monday morning off with a confrontation. Audrey hadn't even made it to the door yet.

Carlene launched herself from the front porch of their office building toward Audrey's car as soon as she had it in park. Carlene didn't to notice the small swarm of crickets hopping madly in her wake.

"I got stuck at the railroad crossing." Ordinarily, Audrey timed her drive to work so that she beat the regular 7:45 a.m. Santa Fe freight train by about five minutes. But she'd overslept this morning. Actually, she hadn't so much overslept as she just couldn't seem to drag herself out of bed.

"What?" Carlene sounded a bit peeved.

Audrey took a deep breath, gritted her teeth, and continued to the porch with Carlene trailing behind. Not the kind of woman who could deal gracefully with bugs of any kind, Carlene had been known to wait in her car until someone else arrived to get rid of them. Ordinarily it amused her to watch Carlene squirm and squeal over something as harmless as a cricket. But today it was just irritating. "I'm sorry I'm late. I didn't beat the train this morning."

Carlene glared at her for a moment. "That's not what I'm talking about."

Audrey grabbed the broom she kept in a corner of the small porch and began to sweep away the nasty brown crickets without even taking her purse from her shoulder.

"That's *not* what I'm talking about." Carlene took the broom from her and dragged her inside by the arm. "*That's* what I'm talking about."

Audrey followed the sight line of Carlene's pointed finger to a vase of flowers set prominently in the middle of her desk.

"Daryl from the flower shop was waiting when I got here. He said these were for you."

"For me?" She grinned. "Who would send me flowers?"

"That's what I thought," Carlene said.

The petite, bright bouquet in the middle of her desk was far too intriguing to even bother with feigning indignation at her friend's remark. Audrey walked around the desk, admiring the bright pinks, yellows, and purples of the flowers.

"I mean, no offense," Carlene continued. "But that's *exactly* what I thought. It's all I could do to keep from snatching the card and reading it myself!"

Audrey stuffed her purse into the bottom drawer and turned the fan on.

"Come on, Miss Smarty Pants."

Audrey arched an eyebrow. "You want to know who these are from?"

Carlene's eyes widened. "Audrey!" She grabbed for the card.

"Just hold on a minute." Audrey snatched the card before Carlene could get it. "Last week you and Jim were all secret smiles for each other, and whenever I asked what was going on, you just smiled and said

'Oh, nothin'. Now, it seems we both want to know something. So maybe we can come to some sort of arrangement, since I am suddenly in a position to negotiate."

Carlene's jaw dropped.

"So tell me. Is there a little something going on between you and Jim?"

Carlene's indignation was tangible, but a slow smile formed anyway. "OK. Yes. Now who are those flowers from?"

"I knew it!" Audrey didn't even try to hide the triumph in her tone. "So what's the story?"

"Oh, no." Carlene shook her head. "I told you what you wanted to know. Now you tell me who those flowers are from."

Audrey opened the envelope that held the card and pulled the little slip out.

I'm really sorry about the rough start last week.
Maybe we could start over?
Brent

Audrey felt her grin fade as she read the message and the signature. She glanced up at Carlene who stood, hands on hips, studying her reaction with narrowed eyes.

"Well?"

"They're from Brent."

Carlene gave a long gasp. "So, what's *your* story?"

"What story?"

"That's what *I'm* askin' *you.*"

"There's no story."

"There's flowers, there's a story," Carlene said. "Did you go out with him this weekend?"

"Was he in town this weekend?"

"Like you don't know!" Carlene's tone bordered

on outrage. She narrowed her eyes again. "Come on. Spill it."

"I can't explain it." Audrey shrugged. "The last time I saw him was last Tuesday. Same as you."

Carlene folded her arms across her chest and sighed. "Then I wonder what he's up to."

"No good," Audrey muttered.

"No doubt," Carlene agreed.

They stood transfixed for a moment by the bouquet on Audrey's desk until the bell on the front door jingled.

"Still quite a few crickets out there," Jim muttered, stepping on a few and then kicking them out the door. He looked up and adjusted his wire-rimmed glasses. "Hey, nice flowers."

"They're for Audrey," Carlene said sweetly. "From Brent Thomason."

"Oh, really?" Jim walked past them toward his office, mock surprise underscoring his words. "By the way, Carlene, did you round up some places to show him? I ran into him at the store yesterday. He said he'd be in first thing this morning. Sounded eager to get settled."

"I sure did." Carlene sent her answer down the hall, following Jim, who didn't wait for a response before heading to his office. "Worked all weekend on it." She rolled her eyes and then glanced over Audrey's flowers again and grinned. "Guess that means you'll get to thank him in person."

"Can't wait." Audrey took the broom and headed out the front door.

As if some cosmic force sought to punish her for sarcasm, Brent's truck turned into the parking lot. She sighed heavily and kept sweeping as his truck door closed. Her heart began to pound in time with his footsteps across the gravel parking lot.

"Good morning." His voice still sounded deep from sleep and so appealing. But the confidence she heard in his tone tempered the sudden longing she felt. It was still just a game to him. An ache rose in her throat, so she tried to clear it away before she spoke.

"Good morning."

"Did you have a nice weekend?"

"I had a fine weekend."

Brent nodded, but continued to stand in the middle of the porch, obviously proud of himself, and clearly expecting something from her.

Audrey tightened her grip on the broom and clenched her teeth. *What's the big idea!* She wanted to shout. *You didn't inflict enough pain and humiliation ten years ago? Thought you'd come on back and twist the knife a little?* She took a deep breath and made a conscious effort to relax. He'd sent flowers. That was all. Whether or not he ever hurt her again was totally up to her.

"Um...thank you for the flowers," she said, finally glancing up at him.

His grin widened. "You're very welcome."

"You really shouldn't have."

Brent nodded and looked down at the keys in his hand. "Maybe." He smiled easily, charmingly. "But I did."

Audrey felt a smile about to touch her own face as her heart inexplicably softened just a little, and she looked down. "Well, thank you."

"You already said that." Brent took a few steps toward her as if he could sense the small crack forming in her defensive wall.

She nodded and turned from him.

The unmistakable sound of hooves scraping and denting metal as Gertie made her way up onto the hood of Audrey's car, thankfully, gave her something besides Brent to focus on. Audrey watched as the goat pawed two or three times at the surface beneath her before dropping her front knees onto it, followed by the rest of her caprine carcass. The goat looked straight at her, brought up some cud, and started chewing. Audrey sighed and resumed sweeping.

"What are you doing for lunch today?" Brent took a couple of steps closer.

"Nothing. I mean, I'll probably run out and pick up lunch for everybody."

"Well, maybe you'd like to let them get their own lunch today, and you and I can run out and get something together."

She stopped sweeping and swallowed hard as her mind reeled. This is just how it started last time. First, he asked her to sit next to him in the cafeteria, then at the basketball game. Next, he was asking her out for a burger at the Prickly Pear after the game. Then it was something about how he'd left his wallet behind at home and could they stop by and get it. It would only take a minute.

She turned to him. "No...thank you."

Brent's grin faded. "Aw, come on, Audrey." His voice was soft, deep and persuasive. Very smooth. He had a way of making that particular phrase, along with a few others, sound as if heartbreak would be imminent if she refused to comply. "As friends."

"Is that what you think we are?" Anger ignited and flashed like gunpowder. "You decide it's time to come home and suddenly we're just old friends no matter what went on between us the last time I saw you. Well, how convenient for you. People who are just friends don't do what we did, Brent."

"No...I—"

"Look, I've got work to do." She turned her back to him, intent on ridding the earth of as many crickets as humanly possible. "Thanks again for the flowers."

"Audrey, you misunderstand me." Brent paused, but she kept sweeping. "I didn't mean to imply that I thought we were just old friends, and that we never...that nothing ever happened between us. Or even that I want something to happen between us again. What I meant was that I hope we can *become* friends. The way we were before...*Better* even."

Audrey sighed and again loosened her grip on the broom, though she fought the urge to go after that stupid goat with it when she heard a demure bleat come from the direction of the car.

"So what do you say?" Brent asked. "Will you have lunch with me today?"

She turned halfway around and glanced sideways at him. It was just lunch. As friends. He seemed so sincere and guileless. And he did send flowers. Surely it wouldn't hurt to budge a little this one time, go to lunch, and catch up on all the years that had passed. What could it hurt?

Audrey looked toward the broom in her hands and caught sight of the scar on the inside of her forearm.

The first time Bobby had shoved her during an argument it had so taken her by surprise that she'd lost her footing and fallen backward over a glass-topped end table, breaking it and cutting a deep gash in her arm in the process. Panic stricken, Bobby had rushed her to the clinic where the doctor gave her a few stitches, and knowingly asked if she wished him to call the police so she could press charges.

She'd been dumbfounded. No, of course she didn't want to press charges. They'd had a fight, Bobby had lost his temper and shoved her a little and she'd fallen. He hadn't meant to hurt her. It had been an accident.

"Audrey?" Brent's quiet inquiry brought her back to the present.

She glanced back to his face and studied it; the strong angle of his jaw, the soft mouth and endearing smile, the hopeful expression in his eyes. Most likely it would hurt if she budged, even this one time. She didn't trust Brent. But he was the least of her worries. Every time she'd fallen for a handsome smile and a charming disposition she'd ended up sorry. Where her judgment was concerned, she couldn't afford to budge an inch.

"Lunch?" Brent questioned.

She shook her head and turned back to her work. "No, thank you."

Somehow he'd managed to blow it with her again.

For a moment, Brent thought he'd convinced Audrey that he truly was interested in her friendship. For a second he could have sworn she was on the verge of accepting his invitation to lunch. But her mind had drifted away to somewhere in their past, no doubt, and she'd come back determined not to give an inch.

Well, good for her.

Brent cast a glance at Carlene, who had shown him three houses already that morning. She'd seemed perturbed at the last one when he said it wouldn't do.

She asked why, but all he could say was that it just wasn't what he was looking for. He'd gladly have told her if he could have.

Now, she drove silently down a deserted farm to market road, and Brent wondered if she might stop the car and tell him to get out.

He smiled. She'd done that to him once. Back in school. And he'd deserved it. She had been driving them home from one of his favorite secluded spots, and he'd told her he didn't want to go out with her anymore.

His reminiscent smile vanished.

"What's so funny?"

Brent shook his head. "Nothing. I was just remembering a time back in school when you dumped me on the side of a road like this one and made me walk back to town."

A grin spread across her features like warm honey. "You got the feeling that's what's fixin' to happen now?"

He shrugged. "It crossed my mind."

"Well, relax," she drawled. "Back then nobody cared who dumped you on the side of the road. Now, since you've come back all educated and respectable, I'd get fired for pulling something like that."

Brent looked out the window as abandoned fields overgrown with parched buffalo grass flew by. There should be more wildflowers this time of year. "So where *are* we going?"

Carlene smiled wickedly and took her time about answering. "The old Denton place is up for sale. It's a good deal, too. It's thirty acres and they're practically throwing the house in for free." She paused and glanced over at him. "The house needs some work, but it's worth the money."

As she turned the car off the paved road and onto a gravel drive he could see the house in the distance, maybe a quarter mile away. From this perspective it looked promising. Carlene parked the car in front with no regard for where the yard used to be.

It was a big old two-story farmhouse. Several coats of white paint had weathered and peeled in subjugation to the elements of summer and winter. What remained was covered with an even coat of dust. A front window had been broken and boarded over, and small fragments of glass still littered the badly sagging front porch.

Carlene had to shove a little to get the door open. Then he followed her across the threshold into the mustiness of an interior that hadn't breathed in awhile.

"It's been sitting empty for a few years." The sound of Carlene's voice bounced around the empty living room. "It wasn't in great shape before that. Still, it's pretty amazing how quickly a house like this'll deteriorate when it just sits empty."

Brent stepped further into the living room, which seemed to come alive with the sunlight and fresh air that poured in behind them. Memories of someone's happy childhood seemed to drift and linger with the breeze as it stirred the dust and the tattered wallpaper. Those imagined memories of roughhousing brothers and giggling sisters quickly mingled with his childhood memories of silence and isolation.

He walked through the living room to the dining room, then on into the kitchen, his footsteps loud and heavy on the old wood floors.

This had been his dream as a child; to live in a big house like this with his mom and a dad and brothers and sisters. He glanced out the kitchen window to the backyard where the rusty skeleton of an old swing set stood. In his mind he saw kids swinging, pushed by their father, perhaps while their mother was inside fixing supper. The harder he concentrated, the clearer he could see himself out there in the backyard, pushing a little blonde haired, green eyed girl as she swung and squealed and demanded to be pushed: *"Higher, Daddy, higher!"*

"This used to be a two-hundred acre cattle ranch." Brent started a little. He hadn't heard Carlene follow him to the kitchen.

"Years ago the Dentons sold most of it off. Now there're a few newer houses out here. But with thirty acres, you'll hardly realize you have any neighbors."

It wasn't that bad. Sure, it was old. And it did need some work. A fresh coat of paint would probably do wonders. The floor could use sanding and refinishing. The roof hadn't looked too great, and the porch was probably beyond help. Even if the foundation needed leveling and the roof needed complete replacement, all of that could be fixed. Not like the old, broken-down mobile home he grew up in.

Afternoons after school and nights he'd always spent alone at home, ever since he could remember. His mother had either been waiting tables somewhere or out with a boyfriend. Periodically, she'd bring one of her boyfriends home, and he'd live with them for a few months or weeks or days. Then she'd be gone again.

Carlene's footsteps startled Brent back to the present. But when he looked at her, for a split second, he saw the girl she had been back then. Sweet, gregarious, popular. Then, a few months later, trying to be so tough as he broke her heart.

"Carlene, I want to apologize for the way I treated you."

The apology sounded abrupt, even to him, but Brent couldn't fight the feeling that the time was right.

Carlene stood frozen, her mouth open, though the words she'd been about to say had vanished. She took a step backward. "What? When?"

"Back in school," he clarified. "The way I treated you."

"Oh." Carlene nodded. "You mean the way you used me for sex then dumped me to chase after someone else."

Brent winced and looked down, but then he nodded. That's exactly what he'd done. He was glad she didn't try to sugar-coat it. He didn't deserve for it to be euphemized. "Yeah. I want to ask you to forgive me."

"What?"

"I mean it," he continued, his voice sounding so meek he almost cringed. "I was such a complete jerk, and you were never anything but good to me. And I'm sorry. Will you forgive me?"

Silence engulfed them for a few moments, and Carlene turned from him, making a show of opening and closing a few cabinet doors. Then she cleared her throat.

"Forget about it," she said, her voice uncharacteristically soft. "It's all part of growing up."

Brent shook his head. "But it shouldn't be. And I'm so sorry that I ever—"

"It's all right, Brent. Forget about it."

"Carlene, I—"

"Brent!"

Yet again, this was not the reaction he had hoped for. But at least Carlene had offered a few conciliatory words. Audrey hadn't even done that. Even so, every fiber of his conscience yearned to say something more, to add a few words that might somehow right his wrongs. But there was nothing more to be said, and Carlene obviously didn't want to discuss it further.

The truth was, a mere apology could never repair the damage he had done all those years ago, to her, to Audrey, to countless other girls, many of whom he was sure he couldn't even remember. Words could never give back what he'd taken from them. But that's all he had to offer. He cast a glance back at Carlene to find her studying him.

"The property is fenced all the way around," she said when he returned his attention to her. "Course, what condition the fence is in I couldn't tell you. There's an old gate at the front drive. It's broken, but you could probably fix it. There's an old barn out back, too. Three bedrooms and one bath upstairs, one bedroom, one bath downstairs. It needs some work."

Brent glanced at Carlene, who began to grin as if she could smell a sale.

"It's a fixer," she concluded.

Brent nodded. "It's perfect."

4

Audrey was useless this morning.

She sighed and tried to blink away the fog in her brain. How many years had it been since anyone sent her flowers? The last bouquet had been a birthday surprise from her mother. Before that, she guessed, the time when Bobby had gone on a particularly violent rampage, demolishing a hollow-core door inside her house, punching several holes in her walls, blackening one of her eyes and, she had thought at the time, cracking a rib or two. She hadn't sought medical treatment. She was never able to face the doctor at the clinic after her initial defense of Bobby. So she lived with the pain and skipped work as many days as possible without arousing too much suspicion.

Bobby had sent a dozen white roses the day of that attack, and had come home later that night with heartfelt apologies and repeated promises to never again lay a finger on her in anger.

Hard as she tried to keep eyes fixed on the computer monitor and her fingers busy typing, she just couldn't stop her attention from wandering back to the blooming vase on the desk.

What on earth had possessed him? With all the women in this town to choose from, it baffled her as to why Brent would choose to bestow his affection, once again, on her. He had to know he wouldn't get very far.

But her infuriating feelings for him were still alive and kicking. Every single time she'd seen him, or even thought about him, that little fluttery feeling exploded in the pit of her stomach. At first she'd hoped it was just nerves, or the feel of her stomach turning at the idea of him. But then it never failed. Her heart would start to hammer, and her face would flush, and all coherent, rational thought would flee her brain for a few seconds while she hoped the years might have changed him for the better.

And Brent always loved a relatively easy challenge. She shook her head and snapped attention back to the computer screen. In that context it made perfect sense. She was probably the easiest target around.

The bell on the front door jingled and she swiveled to greet whoever came in. Carlene, in an obvious daze, strode straight past her desk and into her own office. No taunts about the flowers still on her desk. No commentary on the weather. No wisecracks of any kind whatsoever.

"Carlene?" Audrey followed her friend. "Carlene, are you OK?"

Carlene stood looking out her window. She nodded but didn't speak.

"How do I know this has something to do with Brent?" Audrey crossed to Carlene and laid a gentle hand on her arm. "What's wrong? What did he do?"

Carlene gave a short, blunt laugh and shook her head, apparently trying to control a sudden rush of tears.

Audrey's heart sank.

Brent hadn't changed at all. He hadn't been back

in town three days yet and already he was up to his old tricks, chasing women, pitting friends against each other, and breaking hearts for the fun of it.

"He apologized." The words came out an unsteady whisper, and Audrey craned her neck, certain she had misunderstood.

"What?"

Carlene took a deep breath, held it for a few seconds, then let it out slowly. She seemed to recover instantly. "He apologized."

Suddenly it was all clear as crystal. "Oh, I see." He probably rode around with her all morning, talking in that soft, slow way of his, softening her up little by little. He'd probably lain awake in his hotel room last night planning the perfect time to make his move–it didn't matter who with. He'd say a few sweet, sincere words: *'I'm real sorry about the way I treated you back in school. It was wrong of me. I'm a changed man. Honest. Sure would be nice if you'd forgive me. Maybe have a little lunch with me.'*

"Then what did he do? Ask you to lunch, or the movies, or to be the first guest for a romantic, candle-light dinner at his new house?"

"It wasn't like that." Carlene turned from the window. "He meant it."

This time it was Audrey who gave a blunt laugh. "Yeah, right! He meant it. Please. He's a worm."

Audrey didn't even finish her editorial regarding Brent's character before she stalked back to her desk, grabbed the vase and flowers, then headed for the back door to the trash alley. She flew across the alley, still muttering slanderous things, and emptied the contents of the vase into an open dumpster.

Carlene stood in the doorway, smirking as she

looked from Audrey's face to the vase in her hand.

"Well, there's no point in throwing the vase out. Besides, it's glass. It'll break if I toss it in there." She pushed past Carlene, stopping to shove the vase on a shelf in the storage closet. "He's a worm." She repeated and gave Carlene a pointed look before she stalked back down the hall to her desk.

"Well, anyway," Carlene said, following her. "Now I understand how you felt the other day when you ran into him at lunch."

Audrey picked up a stack of papers and crossed the room to the filing cabinet. Doubtful. Brent may have used both of them in a similar way. They may have been exactly the same to *him*. But Carlene couldn't know how badly his apology had hurt. She couldn't know that Audrey had loved Brent, and had believed him when he'd said he loved her. She couldn't possibly have a clue that deep down she still loved him. The breath caught in her chest, and she pressed her lips together to stifle a sudden rush of tears.

But she shook it off. The idea that what had gone on between them was just water under the bridge, that he felt like he could just sweep back into town and apologize for it and have everything neatly forgiven and forgotten...well, that just made it worse. That just made her mad.

"When you came in all upset about it, I thought you were overreacting just a bit. But now...I don't know. It's hard to imagine an apology affecting me that way. You'd think it would make me feel better, not worse."

Audrey slammed a file drawer and opened the one below it.

"But," Carlene continued, "at least you didn't

actually have sex with him."

Audrey froze in mid-file and blinked. "What?"

"I mean, sure, he may have treated you badly, but at least you didn't let him strip you of all your dignity. So to speak."

She blinked again. "What makes you think we didn't—"

"Oh, now, don't get all defensive." Carlene, quite recovered from whatever confrontation she'd just come from, perched herself on the edge of Audrey's desk and crossed one leg over the other. "Remember, it's a *good* thing you didn't. I'm proud of you. I was proud of you then, too. When I heard you were gonna go out with him, I thought: 'Well, there goes Audrey. Guess no one's safe from him.'

"Kyle Clayton saw him the next morning before he left town and said that Brent didn't have anything to say about your *date*. Not a word. And you know how he liked to brag. We all knew his silence meant that he didn't have anything to brag about."

Carlene paused and pushed a cuticle back. A slow grin spread across her face. "My guess was that's why he left town in such a hurry without a word. He couldn't face his buddies after being shot down.

"But at least he didn't lie about it. He could have told Kyle that he *had* slept with you, then it would have been all over the place even though it wasn't true."

Audrey stood, slack-jawed and blinking, unable to form a complete, coherent sentence in her mind, much less articulate one.

"I, for one, had a lot more respect for you after that." Carlene hopped off the desk and straightened her skirt. "That's when we all realized that all those morals you were so on fire about were more to you than just show. Though it sure surprised me when you hooked up with Bobby Kerr. And it flat out shocked me when he moved in with you. Why'd you do that?"

Audrey shrugged and then stammered. "I...I don't know. Bad judgment. I've yet to pick a winner."

"Yeah, well, join the club." Carlene pushed her hair behind her ears. "Now, if you'll excuse me, I have a seller to contact. Hey, you feelin' OK? You look a little pale."

Audrey nodded and looked at the small stack of papers in her hands. "Yeah. Fine." She turned to resume filing. "You sold him a house?" she asked over her shoulder.

"I think he's going to make an offer on the old Denton place."

"The old Denton place? Is it even still standing?" Audrey turned back around to find Carlene standing in her doorway wearing a triumphant, if sly, grin.

"Serves him right, huh?" Carlene turned and disappeared into her office.

Five minutes ago Audrey would have certainly agreed.

❧

As a kid, Audrey had once seen a T.V. show where a magician snapped a tablecloth off of an elaborately set dinner table–right out from underneath all the china and silver and stemware. Not only did none of it break, but after the trick was completed, every piece remained in its exact original position on the table, as if it had never even been disturbed. The only difference was the tablecloth was gone.

She spent the rest of the day feeling like that table.

Every part of her life was still in its proper place, undisturbed, though a fundamental component was now totally different—gone, in fact.

She tossed purse and keys down onto her kitchen table with a heavy sigh. Believing Brent had said nothing of their time together all those years ago was exceedingly difficult. It had crossed her mind several times that afternoon to ask Carlene if she'd heard their conversation correctly, or if they'd even had the same conversation that she'd been reliving ever since.

The idea that all those pointing fingers and whispers of years ago had been her classmates talking to each other about how she *hadn't* given in to him was almost absurd. Perhaps it hadn't gotten back to Carlene, unlikely as that was. School *had* been over. The usual network of gossip had completely broken down shortly after graduation.

Regardless, someone besides her, Brent, and Bobby, had to know the whole truth. There had been too many eager participants in hushed conversations whenever she'd entered a room for the news about her to have been good. Audrey had always been a nice girl, a good girl. She had always intended to "save" herself for her husband. And she'd been openly proud of that despite the fact that some had ridiculed her for it.

What was it about human nature that led people to rejoice in the failures of others? She had been no different. Rumors would fly, and she'd think the worst of girls like Carlene Fletcher, believing herself to be somehow better. A sorry sounding chuckle escaped before she could check it. It had never occurred to her that she could so easily be added to their ranks.

But fail she did, first with Brent, then with Bobby.

Even after she'd fallen for Brent, her intentions

remained true. She knew what kind of boy he was, but it didn't matter. She'd intended to convert him, to save him from himself, and then to marry him. They'd live happily ever after in her perfect teenage fantasy. She could apply the same exact formula to her relationship with Bobby, too.

She blinked to find herself standing in front of her open refrigerator, the contents of which were about as unappetizing as a three-day-old bean burrito–speaking of which....

Audrey grabbed a plastic bag from the top shelf and opened it to check the viability of the untouched burritos inside. Soggy.

She let the refrigerator door swing closed as she chucked the whole bag into the garbage can by the back door. Then she opened the small pantry to survey its contents. Nothing appealed to her. Maybe later she'd have a bowl of cereal or a sandwich; something cool that didn't require the use of the oven or stove or even the microwave. For now, a cold diet soda would do. She reached back into the fridge for a can, and turned for the living room as she pulled the tab back.

The place was a disaster. She had to step around two laundry baskets full of clothes she'd brought in from the laundromat on Saturday and left in the middle of the floor.

Lately, it seemed, she'd lost the motivation to cook or clean or get up off the couch for much of anything besides work. But tonight she needed to do something besides sit and watch television from six p.m. until midnight.

She pulled a basket of towels onto the couch.

There has to be more to life than this. The hopeless thought slipped through her mind just before a surge of tears came rushing up. *This can't be all there is.*

Audrey shook her head and swallowed the tears back down. "Stop it," she said under her breath. "Just stop."

This was her father's way of coping. Not hers. And she wouldn't give in to it. But as hard as she fought against them when they surfaced, these feelings never subjected themselves to her control. She wiped the tears away and reached for the remote as a knock sounded on her door.

She took a deep breath. *What now?*

She had to suppress a groan when she pulled the door open. *Of course!* She should have known she'd find Brent smiling at her through the screen.

"Hi." An irritatingly cheerful smile lit his features, and despite the new perspective she had gleaned from her earlier conversation with Carlene–maybe even because of it, her first impulse was to slam the door in his face. From the unfeeling way he'd taken advantage of her to the false nobility of his refusal to boast about it, if that was really what had happened, Audrey had reached her limit.

But her heart softened as his expression shifted from carefree playboy to concerned friend. If he had kept his mouth shut all those years ago, for whatever reason, it had been a noble gesture.

"You OK?" His voice sounded tender and sincere.

Audrey nodded.

"You been cryin'?"

"No." That came out sounding belligerent and unconvincing. Although that wasn't how she'd meant it, which was probably just as well. She didn't need him thinking she wanted him here. "How'd you find out where I live?"

Brent laughed as if she'd just said something funny. "Your Dad told me."

"He told you where I live?"

"Yeah. I guess he figured we were old friends so it'd be OK."

There it was again. That grin, more of a smirk, which seemed to mock her and frequently reduced her composure by at least a third. All she could do was fume. And she couldn't even do that very well the way her heart suddenly started to pound.

Even so, the emphasis he'd placed on the phrase "old friends" was ill received after their confrontation on the office porch this morning. Bringing it up again was *so* like him. He could tell it bothered her, too. He looked down and toyed with the keys in his hand.

"Now look, Audrey," he said. "I'm sorry. I didn't think sending flowers would be the wrong thing to do. I thought you might like them. Do you think we could talk without this screen door between us?"

Audrey studied him for a moment. Hard as she tried, there was never any way to discern his motivation. There was no doubt he was trying to finagle an invitation inside. But this was her house, and she didn't intend to let him come in. She pushed the screen door open and stepped out onto the porch.

"What did you want to talk about?"

Brent stammered. "Nothin' in particular. I just thought maybe we could catch up."

"Why me?"

Brent shook his head. "What?"

"Why do you want to catch up with me? There are plenty of other women in this town whom you haven't seen or heard from in years. Heck, there's probably even a few you've never met. Why not one of them?"

Brent stood and blinked at her for a few seconds, his mouth opening and closing as if he were at a loss for words. "Because," he said finally, with a distinctly exasperated edge, "you're the one who's been on my mind all this time."

It was all she could do to keep from rolling her eyes, and she turned to go back inside. But before she could get to the door Brent reached out and touched her arm.

It was a light touch, just a few fingers on her upper arm. But it sent a fire through her, triggering a hundred memories she wished she didn't have, reminding her of other touches and caresses that had meant so much to her and so little to him.

In a move very unlike him, Brent withdrew his hand almost as quickly as he'd reached out to touch her. But it did nothing to stop the flood of images of the two of them together one time, one night, ten years ago.

"Everything OK over there, Audrey?"

She turned to find her next door neighbor standing on his front porch watching them closely. "I'm fine, Mr. Garner. Thank you."

When she turned her attention back to Brent, he continued as if there hadn't been an interruption. "There's something I've wanted to tell you since I decided to come home. Longer than that, actually."

She folded arms across her chest and waited.

He stammered a little before he got started. "I'm not the same guy I was back then."

She widened her eyes, trying to look as innocent as possible. "Back when, Brent?"

He met her gaze briefly before looking down to the keys in his hands. "Back in school."

She shook her head, feigning total ignorance when he glanced up. Let him come right out and say what he'd done.

Brent let go a long breath and nodded, seeming to understand. "When I took advantage of you, Audrey. When I used you for my own gratification. Is that what you want me to say? Or should I be even more specific?"

She looked down and swallowed the rising ache, sorry she'd pushed him.

"My point is," his gentle voice eased the sting, "I'm not that guy, anymore."

"So I've heard."

His answering smile looked quite sad. "Well, it's true. About six years ago I became a Christian."

She felt her jaw slacken, but she didn't let it drop. "A Christian?"

He nodded.

"Of the 'born-again' variety?"

He nodded again, then launched into his story beginning with the phone call from his friend back home, to the drunk cowboy, to the man in the bar parking lot who seemed to read his thoughts. He told the whole story up to the point at which he'd decided to come back home. When he finished, she could only stand and stare at him.

"And you haven't been on a binge since?" The question sounded doubtful even to her.

He shook his head. "I haven't had a drink since."

"And you haven't slept with anyone since?"

Brent shook his head. "No."

Audrey knew she shouldn't laugh. If what he said was true, it took a lot of courage to come here and open up like this. But the ludicrous irony of his words seemed so absurd that she couldn't stop the laughter once it started. She covered her mouth and tried to control herself. To her relief, Brent smiled. Then he looked down again.

"You're laughing at me," he said softly.

"No," Audrey said, as she recovered. "No, not at you."

"Then at what?"

She took a deep breath and stretched a small stitch out of her side. If what he said was true–and it had to be, because not even he was despicable enough to use such a ploy to entice a woman to visit his hotel room. If what he said was true, then the thing she'd wanted most as a girl had come to pass.

Too bad it was too late.

Audrey shook her head. "This was something I prayed for a long time ago. It's just ironic, that's all."

He nodded. "Well, thank you, Audrey. For praying for me. God doesn't always answer our prayers according to our schedule. But He does answer."

Audrey opened her mouth to tell him how she thought God worked nowadays. But she paused. What would she say? That she didn't believe her prayers had much to do with his experience? That she now lived a life so distant from God she wondered sometimes if He had ever listened? That by now He had probably given up on her completely?

She could say those things. And by saying them perhaps she could save him the trouble of finding out the disappointing news the hard way. But she closed her mouth and sighed. She could remember how he felt now, as if life was good, as if God listened, as if God answered prayers.

There is a love that can reform any man.

The idea drifted gently through her mind, as it had that evening on her parents' patio. She knew the truth. She believed. Still, that love didn't move her even though she longed for it to.

Finally she nodded and gave him a melancholy smile.

"There's so much I want to talk to you about," he said, his enthusiasm spilling freely. "Let's go get a burger or something. We can talk over dinner."

Audrey took a step back and shook her head. "I can't. I'm really not feeling all that well tonight. I might just lie on the couch and watch T.V., then go to bed early."

He nodded. "OK. Tomorrow then."

She sighed. "Brent, I..."

"I guess you've probably never been treated right by a man. I don't blame you for not trusting me. But I don't know how to make it any clearer. I'm not that guy anymore. I don't have ulterior motives."

She shook her head and reached for the handle of the screen door.

"Please, Audrey. Just dinner. Just a burger at the Prickly Pear. New times, not old times."

What was wrong with her? Hadn't she learned anything from her past relationship with this man? He might claim to be a Christian now, but that didn't guarantee he'd really changed. When presented with an opportunity to take advantage he might easily revert back to his former self. Her faith certainly hadn't prevented *her* from making the worst mistakes of her life. And she obviously still had no control where he was concerned.

Even now, knowing what she knew about him,

knowing how he'd been and probably could be still, she wanted nothing more than to fall into his arms, for him to cover her with kisses and tell her that he loved her.

What was wrong with her?

The words were still bouncing around inside when she felt her head nod and heard her faint assent to his invitation.

"Tomorrow, then," Brent said with that devastating smile of his. "Seven o'clock."

5

Brent had been every bit the gentleman so far.

Audrey bit her lower lip and shot a covert glance in his direction. He looked relaxed in the way that people get after eating a little too much and enjoying a pleasant conversation with a good friend. He leaned back against the seat and was steering his truck with one hand, the other resting on his thigh. She let her gaze travel back up to his profile, letting her mind wander back over the details of their time together.

"You look good." Those had been his first real words to her after they'd ordered their meals at the Prickly Pear.

She had redirected her attention from spreading the paper napkin to him. "What?"

"You look good." He leaned forward, folding his forearms on top of the table. His smile had been lazy as he drawled his next words. "The years haven't been cruel to you."

It had taken her a moment to realize he wasn't kidding. But the realization slowly dawned along with a sincere smile. Of all the things she could recall about him from their younger days, sparkling wit wasn't one of them. And, while that exchange may not have been particularly inspiring, it had in its own way been quite flattering. She had felt the blush as it crept upwards to cover her face

Audrey felt it rising again right now. She pressed cool palms to her warm cheeks and turned to look out the window.

It had gone well. Better than she expected. The conversation had been friendly if at times a little awkward. Three times, some old buddy had stopped by their booth just to say hello and give him a wink and a nudge of encouragement. Apparently word was out about how she was treating him, and he inspired admiration for his perseverance. He always had.

As much as she wanted to, Audrey couldn't honestly say she hadn't enjoyed their outing. He had always known how to make a girl feel special, and the years had only served to enhance his skill. He listened more now. He seemed earnestly interested in everything she had to say despite the fact that what she'd talked about probably would have bored most men to tears and they would've sent a quick signal to the waitress for their check.

He had spoken enthusiastically about his faith and his new job, as if his new boss weren't her father. For moments here and there it had felt as if they were friends.

Audrey glanced back at Brent again, any level of comfort she had achieved tonight stealing away as he steered his pickup to the curb in front of her house and brought it to a gentle stop.

Before he even had time to shift into park she pushed the door open and slid out. "Well, thanks for dinner. I had a good time."

Maybe if she acted like all she expected was for him to drop her off she could make it to the door and inside without having to deal with the traditional end of the date hassle. She tried to blink away an image of him sliding arms around her and pressing a soft kiss to her mouth. She *tried* to. But the image threatened to turn into a full blown daydream almost as quickly as it materialized.

Audrey pushed the door closed, turned sharply, and headed up the sidewalk to her porch. About halfway there his engine stopped. He intended to follow her. She let out an irritated breath. *Great.* This was the last thing she needed; trying to escape another invitation, not to mention any physical contact with him, and him pursuing it.

His door slammed and she dove into her purse, looking for her keys by the dim bulb burning above. She could hear everything; the slow pulsating drone of the cicadas, a dog barking down the street, the soft papery sound of the moths above as they flew repeatedly into the hot light bulb. Then she heard his footsteps, slow and deliberate on the concrete, and the jingle of his keys. She gritted her teeth as she continued to search for her own elusive set. They were in there somewhere. She gave her purse a shake. She could hear them.

Finally her hand found the cold hard steel that would facilitate her escape. She yanked open the screen and unlocked her door.

"You ought to at least let a man open the door for you." His voice was warm and his tone teasing as he spoke practically right into her ear. He reached around her to hold open the screen.

Audrey started and stepped quickly into her living room through the now open front door. "Sorry. Just thought I'd save you the trouble of getting out."

"It's no trouble."

She nodded, dropped her purse and keys into a

frayed chair by the door, and turned around. But Brent just stood there at the threshold watching her. "You're letting moths in."

"Clearly, that's an invitation inside." He stepped in, letting the screen door close softly before pushing the front door closed.

She followed his gaze around the room, suddenly seeing it as if through someone else's eyes. The walls had been patched in a few places but never repainted after Bobby's rampages. She saw the mismatched furniture, the old carpet, the general lack of decent housekeeping. She felt the stuffy, stale air, barely stirred at all by the one window unit in this room.

Shame stung, although she didn't know exactly why. "I'm really not such a slob." She looked down. "It's just been too hot to do too much, and I wasn't expecting to have a visitor tonight."

Brent stepped across the room and placed the palm of his hand against one of the wall's patched spots. "Looks better than my place."

She nodded. "The Denton place? I'll bet it does."

"I'll get it fixed up though." He smoothed his hand across the surface of the wall, then crossed back to her.

"Oh, wow!" He slipped past her and picked up a high school yearbook from the coffee table. "I haven't seen this in..." He dropped himself onto her couch. "Has it really been ten years?"

Audrey recognized it for the rhetorical question and said nothing.

He flipped the cover open and thumbed through the pages. "It's strange how I feel like my life is just now beginning."

She looked down and moved to sit in a chair

adjacent to him. *Must be nice to feel like you can just start over. To forget everything you've done up until now.* She nearly choked trying to suppress the words. She cleared her throat. "I meant to ask you earlier. How's your mother doing?"

He took a deep breath, then shrugged and snapped the annual closed. "I don't know. I haven't talked to her in three or four years. I don't even know where she is now."

Audrey looked down and picked at a frayed spot on the arm of the chair. "Oh. I'm sorry."

"She's known where I've been. She could just as easily have called me. More so even, since I wasn't moving in with someone new every few months."

The bitterness in his voice was barely detectable. But it was there, and it surprised her. She cast a sideways glance just to see if there was any trace of it in his expression. In all the years she'd known him she'd never heard him say a critical word about his mother. Her promiscuous behavior had never been a secret and had even been at the center of several virulent rumors. But he never mentioned it. And she had never perceived the least bit of hostility in him. He had always been so easy-going and carefree. Nothing bothered him.

She glanced away when his eyes met hers.

"Not that it really matters." His tone had returned to normal again. "It's not like she was ever all that interested in me."

"Because you're a Christian, now?"

He looked at her and squinted. "Hmm?"

"Is that the reason you and she aren't speaking?"

He shook his head. "Nah. I don't think so. I don't think she really cares one way or the other about that.

She laughed when I told her."

Audrey looked down again, feeling as if she'd just been slapped. She swallowed as a lump began to form in her throat. His faith was important to him. The majority of his conversation this evening had been illustrated by it. But now, all she could remember was their conversation just yesterday evening when he had stood on her front porch and bared his faith to her for the first time. And she laughed, too.

"Brent, I'm sorry." Her voice sounded small and tight.

He shrugged. "It's really not that big a deal."

"No, I mean I'm sorry that I...because I..." She glanced back up at him, unable to finish.

His expression softened. "Because you laughed, too?"

She focused again on the frayed spot on the arm of her chair.

"Not the same. Besides which, I'm pretty sure that my mother never prayed for my salvation."

"Still, I—"

"Audrey." He stopped her argument with his voice and she glanced at him again, needing more evidence that she hadn't behaved just like his mother. "You really cared for me. You prayed for me, and you had faith in me. You had faith that I would change. That's more interest than anyone else ever took in my welfare. And we both remember clearly how I behaved despite the fact that I knew all about your principles. Your cynicism last night didn't surprise me. It didn't offend me, either."

Audrey blinked back tears and glanced down at her hands. What was it that she felt for this man? Everything he said was true. He had known how she felt, that she had loved him. At least as much as she thought possible back then. He had known of her faith, and that he was a temptation she wouldn't try very hard to resist. He had preyed on that, and that had been a snake-in-the-grass low thing to do. Yet the idea that *she* might have hurt *his* feelings brought tears to her eyes.

She drew a deep breath and looked up to find him studying her. If she hadn't been sure before, the look in his eyes left no remaining doubt that he was a different man now. His faith was true. She so wanted to be happy for him, to rejoice with him. But her faith was so feeble.

"Well," he said finally, pushing up off the couch. "I should go."

Audrey stood and followed him to the door. Before reaching for the knob, he turned to face her and she looked down, embarrassed by the tears in her eyes.

"Audrey." The tenderness in his voice made the breath catch in her throat. It was all she could do to keep from leaning into his touch when he reached out to brush her hair away from her face. "What's wrong?"

A tear fell as she closed her eyes against the fiery tenderness of his touch and his sincere entreaty for her trust. She shook her head, gathering what little strength she had, and backed away from him.

"Can I see you again soon?" He inched toward her, lessening the gap she'd put between them.

She shook her head again.

"Just dinner. We don't have to go fast. The slower the better as far as I'm concerned. Please, say you'll see me again."

"I can't."

"You can."

"No, I can't. Thanks for dinner, Brent. I really did have a nice time. I enjoyed catching up. But I—"

"Why not?"

"Because...I just can't. I don't want to."

"Audrey—"

"I have always done this wrong." She snapped the words through her constricted throat. "Starting with you. I can't even hear your name without remembering every mistake I ever made..." She let her voice trail off when the injured look on his face registered. Another tear fell. "I'm sorry."

"No," he said quietly, "I'm sorry."

Already she wanted to take the words back. They were all true, and she didn't think she could bear seeing him again. But she didn't want to hurt him either.

"Brent, I—"

He raised a hand and shook his head. Then he stepped forward, closing the gap between them completely, took her hand and pressed her palm to his chest, over his heart. It was as if he were struggling to contain a rush of words and a rush of tears all at the same time. Part of her desperately wanted him to lose the struggle and say everything that was in his heart. Another part of her just wanted him to go.

"I did this to us, Audrey." His voice was thick and as charged with emotion as she'd ever heard it. "I ruined my chance with you years ago, I know that. I just thought maybe..." He let his voice trail off and shook his head. Finally he let go of her hand and nodded again. "It's not your fault."

He turned and left her house without another word, but the disquiet rising up inside made her want to cry out loud.

రెల్

The halogen lights of the convenience store's parking lot lit Blithe Settlement's night sky with blinding intensity. Three times in the past twenty minutes Brent had grabbed the handle of his truck door intent on going in for a six-pack, and three times he'd drawn his hand back and raked it through his hair.

It was just a six-pack. What difference could it make?

A few years ago, one six-pack would have barely gotten him started. Maybe he'd just buy one bottle. Just enough to relax a little and maybe dull the ache that had once again begun to nag at his heart.

After he left Audrey's he drove out to what would soon be his own home. He hadn't closed the deal yet, so he didn't have a key. But as the evening's dusky blues and corals yielded to indigo and finally the Milky Way, he toured the outside of his property, locating the old hay barn and the gate that Carlene said had been removed from the fence long ago.

He sat on the front porch for an hour replaying the scene with Audrey. Hurting him hadn't been her intention when she'd said she couldn't even hear his name without regret. But her rejection had, nonetheless, hurt badly. Doubly so considering that rejection was exactly what he deserved from her.

Brent hadn't come back intending to pursue her. But when he'd seen her that very first day in the Prickly Pear, he'd known that a relationship with her, even if it was just a rekindling of their former friendship, was what he wanted most.

Before she'd become just another object of conquest for him she'd been one of his few true friends. Maybe his only one. She had been sweet, honest, sensitive. The complete opposite of him. He didn't know why he suddenly turned on her and treated her so dishonorably. He couldn't explain it.

Since they'd been children, Audrey had been the most stable, unchanging presence in his life. In elementary school, she had shared her lunch with him when his mother had neglected to pack him one, which was most every day. Early on in their high school days, she'd helped him pass a few classes in which he was struggling so that he could remain eligible to play football before he quit caring altogether. She'd been the smart one, and would have excelled in college.

It saddened him to find her still here, working at a job that didn't suit her, living in a house with badly patched walls and dingy carpet that was little better than the trailer he grew up in.

It was almost as if they had exchanged lives.

Brent came home with a college education and a good job in the profession of his choice, yearning for a family of his own despite the fact that it was the last thing he deserved.

But Audrey seemed aimlessly adrift, alone, living day-to-day, terribly unhappy and seemingly determined to stay that way. He had no way of knowing what all had happened to her after he'd gone. But she'd made it clear that her involvement with him had been her most regrettable wrong choice. It made him feel like he had laid the foundation for all her other bad choices. He probably had.

A big, dark, diesel four by four rumbled into the parking lot and startled him back to the present. He finally opened his door and stepped out. This was the last place he ought to be right now. He should turn around, get back into his pickup and drive away. The feeling almost overwhelmed him, and for a second he stopped and halfway turned. Then her words drifted back to him.

I can't even hear your name without remembering every mistake I ever made.

He pressed on toward the door.

"Hey, Brent!" A cheerful voice greeted behind the checkout counter as he walked in.

Kyle Clayton, one of his best buddies back in school, had been the one who had kept him caught up on all the information back home. Kyle, who, back in high school, would occasionally circumvent the policy of the Four Star Motel and get him a room for an hour or two, was at work behind the register. It had been a year since he'd spoken with him. Apparently he'd changed careers.

"I heard you were back in town," Kyle said. "I was wonderin' when I was gonna hear from you."

Brent stepped up to the counter and shook Kyle's hand.

"What brings you in?"

"I thought I'd stop off for a little something to drink."

"Good. Good. Beer's always on sale here."

Brent nodded and looked around.

"It's cheaper by the case!" came a voice from behind him.

Bobby Kerr stepped up to the counter and heaved two cases onto it.

Bobby was two or three years older than him. Even in his early thirties, his close-cropped, dark brown hair was beginning to show signs of gray at the temples. He was a complete undesirable as far as Brent was concerned. But it wasn't impossible to see why a woman might be attracted to him. His skin was tanned, and his frame lean and muscular. He was always well-dressed and usually clean-shaven, though now he wore a trendy beard around his mouth and chin. He had unusual, light-brown eyes and his disposition was disarmingly friendly, volatile, and unpredictable.

"If it ain't Brent Thomason." Bobby was probably already half drunk. But he could hold his alcohol better than most, and Brent couldn't remember ever seeing him any other way. "How long you been back in town?"

"A few days." Brent clenched his jaw.

"You come home to break some more hearts, buddy?"

"I came back for a job."

"A job?" Bobby sounded as if the concept had never occurred to him. "What kind of job?"

"I'm a vet. I took a job at the Rhodes' clinic."

"Speakin' of the Rhodes'. Has anyone seen Audrey lately? She still living over on Third Street? Seems I'm in need of a place to hang my hat for awhile."

Brent clenched his jaw and glanced at Kyle, who returned a nervous look, then cleared his throat. "I don't think she's gonna take you back, Bobby. Seems she's seeing Brent here now."

Bobby looked from Kyle to Brent. "That true?"

"Yeah." Brent looked Bobby in the eye, not even trying to cover the challenge he knew showed on his face.

Bobby nodded and smiled casually, but his irritation was almost tangible. "Well, then, I guess I'll have to find someplace else to stay. For now." He opened his wallet, pulled out enough cash to cover his purchase and replaced it with the change. "Guess I'll see y'all around."

"So, things are off to a pretty good start for y'all." A smile had spread across Kyle's face while Brent watched Bobby step into the noisy diesel.

Brent turned back to Kyle and shook his head. Then he went to survey the coolers at the back of the store.

"You mean she shot you down again?"

What had he been thinking when he asked her to dinner? That she'd thank him for coming back to her? That simply telling her he had changed would be enough to convince her that he was finally worthy of her love? Was he?

Brent opened a cooler and reached in for a cold six-pack.

"So tell me, what are you gonna do next? You gonna ask her out again? I hear the third time's the charm. Or hey, what about Carlene Fletcher? That one's easy on the eyes, that's for sure. Course, Carlene and Audrey are friends now, so that might just cause a whole lot of trouble you'd probably rather avoid. You know, if you play your cards right, maybe Audrey'll come around. She's a nice woman, a pretty one, too."

Kyle paused and reflected. "After she threw Bobby out I thought maybe I'd ask her for a date. But till recently she just always seemed so sad. But it's only a matter of time for you, right?"

Brent set the beer down on the counter and reached for his wallet. He shrugged good-naturedly and gave Kyle a confident smile that contradicted every emotion he currently felt.

"Just a matter of time," he said, tossing a few bills onto the counter.

Kyle grinned as he rang up the sale and handed Brent his change. "It's gonna be good having you back in town, man. Just like old times, huh?"

Just like old times.

The words echoed through the chambers of Brent's mind and stung his heart like an unexpected slap. *Just like old times.* He looked down at the change in his hand and the six pack on the counter.

God, what am I doing?

This was not what he wanted. This was not him anymore. This hadn't been how he dealt with his setbacks in years. *What am I doing?*

"Brent? Buddy?" Kyle's voice edged its way into his consciousness. "You OK?"

Brent blinked and cleared his throat, setting his handful of change on the counter and sliding it across to Kyle. "I changed my mind."

Kyle's eyes narrowed into an expression communicating utter confusion. "What?"

"I don't want to buy this. Just give me my money back."

Kyle moved slowly to carry out Brent's request, as if giving him time to come to his senses. "What's goin' on?"

"Nothing." Brent shoved the bills back into his wallet, then stuffed it into his back pocket. "I just changed my mind."

Kyle took a deep breath and shook his head. "Ooookay."

"I quit drinking six years ago. I'm not gonna start again now just because I had one disappointing night." Brent looked for signs of understanding on the other guy's face, but found none. "See you around."

A disdainful chuckle followed him as he headed for the door. "Yeah, man. Maybe in church."

Brent paused and expelled a weary breath before pushing the door open. Outside the halogen lights beat down like a spotlight as he hurried to his truck.

6

It wasn't a hangover. It couldn't be.

Brent clearly remembered asking for his money back and pushing the beer back across the counter to Kyle. He remembered leaving empty handed. More than anything he remembered Kyle's scornful laugh. It still echoed inside his head in perfect rhythm with the dull, throbbing ache at his temples.

It wasn't a hangover. Brent took a deep breath, trying to tamp down the mild queasiness that rolled through him as the pain in his head briefly intensified. But it sure felt like one.

Brent sat on the edge of the hotel bed and buried his face in his hands for a moment before raking them through his hair. His gaze fell on the phone that sat only an arm's length away. It was seven o'clock. Pete Daly, his friend and pastor back in College Station, would be up by now. He could call.

But for what? To fish for support? To confess the weakness he'd felt last night? To cry? To hear someone say he wasn't the worthless loser that he knew deep down he was?

"God, what am I doing here?" The prayer came out of his parched throat sounding more like a croak.

Coming here had probably been the stupidest thing he'd ever done. What had possessed him to believe that it might be a good idea? A few weeks back he might have said God was prompting him to come home.

God, how could I have been so completely wrong?

Brent closed his eyes and gritted teeth against the fresh surge of pain when he stood. Then he uttered a bitter laugh. Rotten as he felt now, he might as well have had that beer last night.

A shower, a shave, and a change of clothes did little to alter his disposition. A few aspirin seemed to go a little further, as did a cup of coffee and a doughnut from the cramped motel lobby. The coffee was barely warm, but it was just as well because the morning was already hot and still.

Sweat filmed his face and neck by the time he arrived at work, and he stepped out of his pickup brushing crumbs from his shirt and jeans. He tossed what was left of the coffee into a patch of dried up weeds and crumpled the paper cup.

At the sound of Lyndon's cheerful greeting he turned to find the elder man and an assistant examining the hind end of a highly agitated and very pregnant Hereford. He expelled a deep breath, waved, and continued on his way into the clinic, stopping by Lyndon's small office, which doubled as a lounge, as there was always a fresh pot of coffee on top of a filing cabinet. He poured a cup and took a slow sip, closing his eyes, letting the liquid do its best to wake him up.

"You feelin' OK this morning?"

Brent started at the unexpected sound of Lyndon's voice. "I'll be fine. Just a headache. What's the trouble with the Hereford?"

"No trouble, really. It's just about her time and that one always needs a little help. The owners are out of town for the week. We'll board her and see what happens."

Brent nodded.

"So what's the status on your house?"

"We're supposed to close on Friday." Brent raked a hand through his hair and then rubbed the back of his neck. "I'll probably start moving in this weekend. Any way I could convince you to let me borrow a trailer?"

Lyndon nodded absently then began shuffling through an array of papers on his desk. "There was a call after you'd gone home yesterday. I wrote down the message. Here."

Brent took the slip of paper and read it.

Wanda Thomason called. She'll call you back.

"She didn't leave a number."

Brent looked up from the note to find Lyndon studying him. With a sigh and a shrug he crumpled the note. "I guess she'll call back when she can. You need some help outside?"

"Why don't you come have a look and tell me what you think."

On his way out the door Brent tossed his mother's message into the trash can beside Lyndon's desk.

ॐ

Smoky haze and the scent of burning grass and mesquite were becoming disturbingly common. Audrey reached out to adjust her air vent, and turned down the volume on the radio when the afternoon news report ended and a loud country song began.

Three hundred fifty acres. That's what the reporter had just said. Three hundred fifty acres had burned in this county alone last week. *Last week.* She shook her head, trying to remember the numbers he'd just rattled off for other counties around here before ending the report with a reminder of the region wide burn ban.

Audrey's mind drifted to the story Carlene had told her today about a grass fire at her father's ranch, started by a spark from a train as it rode along the track that bordered his land. She blew out a breath and turned the fan on her air conditioner up, hoping it might, by some miracle, start cooling again. All this talk of wildfires and drought only seemed to make it hotter. But the smoky smell in the air as she turned her car off Main Street and onto her road wasn't a product of her imagination. Somewhere nearby, someone's property was burning.

Thankfully, no flames engulfed her home. But an unfamiliar shiny, black four by four parked on the front curb stirred an uneasiness that made her heart jump. There was no one in it, and no one hanging around outside. It probably belonged to the visiting friend of a neighbor. But a distinctly bad, almost menacing feeling began to nag as she approached her front door.

The feeling proved true when she realized the front door was already open. Then the screen door began to swing out, as if in slow motion, guided by a hand she was all too familiar with.

"Surprise, baby! I'm home!" Bobby Kerr stepped out and stood on her front porch like a bad dream, arms open wide, with a long neck bottle in one hand and a cheap convenience store bouquet in the other. The sight took her breath, and not in a good way.

Audrey stopped short in the middle of her front yard wishing desperately there were something solid to reach for. She blinked once, twice, trying to make the vision go away. But it didn't. "How did you get into my house?"

"I just let myself in." Bobby took a slow sip from the bottle, and let the hand with the flowers drop to his side.

"You just broke in, you mean." She steeled herself. This was really happening. Quick as she could, she gathered her scattered wits. *What would a smart woman do in this situation?*

"I didn't break in, it was unlocked."

Before he even had time to finish his statement, Audrey turned and started for her next-door neighbor's house. She wanted to drop everything and run like mad, but she kept remembering what her father always told her about dealing with an aggressive dog.

Don't touch it. Don't tease it. Don't even go near it. Don't run from it, it'll chase you, and don't let it know that you're afraid of it. Stand your ground.

She should have run.

Bobby was at her side instantly, and his grip on her arm was quite firm, if not quite violent. "Hey, where you goin'?"

"To call the police."

"Baby, wait—"

"Audrey!" She snapped the word and gave an experimental tug to see if she could free her arm from his grasp. It didn't budge. "My name is Audrey!"

"Audrey, honey, can't we just sit and talk for awhile. What's it been? Nearly a year? We've got a lot of catching up to do." His voice was soft and persuasive, and his eyes pleaded with her. But she could feel his fingertips contradicting his gentle demeanor as they dug deeper into her flesh.

"Don't touch me!" Audrey gritted teeth and wrested her arm from his grasp, taking several large steps backward. If she could just put a big enough gap between them, keep out of his reach, then she could make a run for Mr. Garner's front door. Bobby had obviously already been drinking, too. So she could probably outrun him. If she could put enough space between them.

Luckily, Bobby took a step backward too, widening her safety zone a little further. But the look on his face expressed hurt, shame, and sympathy all at the same time. She had to look away. She cast her gaze down to the expanse of brown grass between them.

"I...I'm not gonna hurt you, Audrey." His voice sounded soft and wounded. Audrey took another step backward. "And I didn't break in. The door was unlocked. I know you're not inclined to trust me, and with good reason. But, baby, you throwing me out was probably the best thing anyone ever did for me. I'm not the same man I was. You just gotta give me the chance to prove it to you."

Audrey watched his boot clad feet as he took a tentative step closer. But when she countered by taking another two steps backward he stopped where he stood. "Being alone for so long, it made me think. About how I was. About how bad I treated you, sometimes."

Tears stung her eyes, and she bit her tongue in an effort to stop them.

"But I'll never hurt you again, baby. I won't hit you or slap you or push you around. I don't want to be that kind of man anymore. And I won't be. Just give me a chance. You'll see."

"I see you're still drinking." Audrey raised her

gaze to the half finished bottle he set down on her porch in his haste to catch her. She folded arms across her chest. *No!* She'd heard this same speech, almost word for word, at least a dozen times. She should be immune.

But why couldn't he change? *Why couldn't he just change?* He had the potential to be such a good man if he would just quit drinking. Lots of people did it. Brent had done it. Why not him? Why did all the years she spent with him have to be for nothing?

"Not as much," he said, obviously taking her response as an invitation to move in a step closer. "And I'll quit drinking. I'll completely quit if you want me to. If it'll prove to you that I mean what I'm sayin'."

"You'll quit drinking," she echoed his words doubtfully.

Bobby nodded.

"Completely." She raised her tearful gaze to his face.

Bobby nodded again.

"And what about Saturday nights with your buddies?"

"What buddies?" Bobby flashed his most charming and sincere grin as he moved closer still. "I wanna be a family man, Audrey. Just think. We could finally make it official. Remember how we used to talk about getting married? We just never did get around to it." He reached out and gently took her hand. "Come on, baby. You know it wasn't all bad with me. We had some good times, didn't we?"

As if through a will of their own her fingers tightened around his. It hadn't all been bad. When he wasn't half-drunk, they actually got along well. It felt like a real marriage. Plenty of times she'd almost convinced herself it was one.

"Remember the day we first got together?" He reached for her other hand, and she felt a reluctant smile touch her mouth. Something about him had reminded her so much of Brent that first night. There was something so easy going and charming in the way he just slid into her booth at the Prickly Pear with his supper and started talking to her like they'd always been friends. He applied no pressure, made no demands. Totally opposite of the way Brent had treated her.

"Don't you remember how we just sat and talked?" The soft promising sound of his voice made her eyes drift closed. "Let's do that again, baby. Let's just go on down to the café and get us some supper and talk for two or three hours. Just like we did the first time. We could start completely over. And do it right this time."

She opened her eyes and studied his face as his hands closed around hers in a gentle squeeze.

"We'll do it right this time. We'll go get you a ring. We'll be engaged for six months or so, so you can plan a wedding like you want. We'll get married, baby. Just like you wanted."

Just like she wanted. Audrey squeezed her eyes shut tight and felt tears fall. She'd never have the wedding she wanted. No way on earth would her father walk her down the aisle and give her to Bobby. No way.

His living with her had been a constant source of contention between her and her parents. The few times they'd actually tried to intervene on her behalf she'd mindlessly taken Bobby's side. Months at a time would pass without so much as a single word being spoken between them because, when they did talk, invariably they'd bring up the subject of her cohabitation and tell her what she needed to do to fix the situation.

Part of her, ashamed and humiliated, had just wanted them to butt out. Another part had wanted to pack up her things and run home. Especially after the violence started. But she'd made her own bed.

Now Bobby stood so close she could smell the familiar masculine fragrance of his cologne. And the beer on his breath. He searched her with his warm, caramel eyes.

"Just give it some thought." His voice was soft and smooth. "We don't have to decide anything right now. Course, there's somethin' you'll need to do for me if I'm gonna be making all these changes to win you back."

Audrey blinked. How had he managed to get so close?

"You'll need to stop running around with Brent Thomason."

"What?" The word came out sharply pointed as she withdrew her hands from his.

"I bumped into him last night at the quick stop. He made it sound like he was planning on moving in here himself."

"What?"

"I mean, I can understand you needing a little companionship and all, but Brent? He'll just be gone again as soon as he gets what he wants from you, baby. Just like last time. Remember?"

Audrey nearly gasped. Why didn't he just go ahead and slap her? Get it over with. "I think you need to leave now." She turned back for Mr. Garner's house. "Now!"

Quick as a flash, Bobby reached out and grabbed her by the arm again, and spun her around to face him. Brent's pickup was slowing to a stop behind Bobby's. An instant later she heard Mr. Garner's front door open.

"Everything OK, Audrey?" Mr. Garner called from his porch.

"No!" She tried again to wrench her arm free from Bobby's grasp. "No, Mr. Garner everything's not OK!"

"Baby, I'm the one who loves you. I miss you." Bobby's voice was urgent, though he made sure that only she would hear his words. "I want to come home."

"Audrey, do you want me to call the police?"

Bobby let go of her arm and stepped away from her. "That's all right, Mr. Garner. That won't be necessary. I was just leavin'." He took a few more steps back, and pointed at her. "I'll call you later and we'll talk about this, OK?"

Without waiting for her response, Bobby turned and headed back to his pickup, not even acknowledging Brent as he went.

Brent watched his truck retreat before he turned and started toward her. "I was just driving by on my way back to the motel."

Audrey didn't wait for him before retreating to her front porch.

"Should I call the police?"

Mr. Garner still stood on his front porch, eyeing Brent suspiciously.

She smiled and shook her head. "No, thank you, Mr. Garner. I'll be OK."

Her neighbor nodded, waved and disappeared into his house.

"Welcome home." Her trembling hands contradicted her levity, and she clasped them together to cover the most obvious indicator of her mental state. "Never a dull moment."

"You OK?"

Audrey nodded and nearly collapsed as she sat on the top porch step. She picked up the bouquet Bobby had left behind in his haste. It had seen better days, and just like the flowers Brent sent, would end up in the garbage.

"He always does this." She tossed the flowers aside. "He always makes a scene right out here in front of everyone and makes me feel like some kind of trailer trash."

Brent laughed ironically. "You? Never. Now, me, on the other hand...."

"Oh, Brent." She almost groaned. "I'm sorry. I didn't mean—"

"It's OK." Brent held up a hand to silence her apology. "I know you didn't mean anything by it."

Audrey sighed, picked up Bobby's half finished beer and examined the label. "Bobby said he ran into you at the convenience store last night."

He looked down at his boots.

"He said you made it sound like you were fixing to move in with me. You didn't happen to say anything like that, did you?"

Brent shook his head and shrugged. "I don't know. I don't remember. I might have led him to believe that you and I were seeing each other. But, honestly Audrey, he was asking about you like he was gonna come straight here. I figured if he thought you were seeing someone else he might at least think about it for a day or so."

Audrey smiled and patted his hand where it rested. She watched his gaze linger on her hand for a long moment until finally she drew it back uncomfortably. "I guess I should thank you for that. I'm sure you spared me having to deal with him last night in the privacy of my own home with no neighbors looking out for me. You should know, though, this all just gives him a reason to beat both of us senseless at some point."

"I guess we'll just have to stick together, then. I don't figure he can take the two of us at once."

Slowly, Audrey tipped the bottle, spilling its contents onto the dried up grass that used to be her front lawn. "The only time he ever used to hit me was after he'd had too much to drink. Aside from that, things were usually pretty good between us." She paused and sighed. "He said he would quit drinking if I wanted him to."

Brent sat silently for so long that she wondered if he heard her. She opened her mouth to repeat it, but stopped before any words came out. He'd heard her. She set the empty bottle down and raised a hand to rub her eyes. How was it possible that she was considering taking Bobby back? After everything he'd put her through, after every time he'd come to her with the same old story, why did she so need him to be telling the truth this time?

"Don't believe him." Brent's voice sounded hoarse. "He won't change."

"You did." Her words barely stirred the air, but she could tell they affected him. He took a deep breath and his Adam's apple rose and fell as he swallowed.

"He *hasn't* changed."

She sighed and nodded. She knew. In her head,

she knew. But her heart had never listened to reason. "Brent," she said softly, "my house isn't on the way to the motel. Why did you stop by?"

He met her gaze for a second, then looked away and shrugged. "I just wanted to check on you. To make sure you were OK. I just had a feeling I should."

The pain she inflicted on him last night was still there and just as fresh. As was her remorse. And for a moment Audrey thought she could take it back. It would be easy to tell him that she'd reconsidered, and she wanted to see him again. If nothing else, it would be the truth. Certainly keeping Bobby at bay would be easier if she had Brent around to defend her, and he would.

But then she'd have him to deal with, and that would create a whole different set of problems. When he left her, Bobby would probably still be hanging around. Ultimately, she'd just be postponing the inevitable.

"Well. Thanks," she said after a long silence. "Thanks for checking on me."

"I should be going." Brent stood abruptly. "Call me if you need anything."

"I will." She looked straight past him. In her peripheral vision she saw him return to his truck.

Postponing the inevitable. Setting herself up for yet more heartache. That's all she'd be doing if she called him back.

7

Audrey hadn't even turned the ignition off before Gertie had her front hooves up on the bumper of her car. She'd overslept again and got stuck behind the train again. She was pleasantly surprised to find that Carlene had apparently made peace with the crickets and gone inside despite the fact that Audrey hadn't swept the porch yet. She was flat out shocked when she got to the front porch and found that someone had already done cricket duty this morning.

Audrey stared at the porch for a moment. Jim must have done it. No way would Carlene put herself in a position to be jumped on by a bug. It didn't really matter. It was a small thing, and the tone of her day turned for the better because of it.

She stepped inside, stopping short at the sight of Carlene perched on her usual corner of the desk, and Jim standing beside her. No, not just standing beside her, but leaning so close their shoulders touched as he finished whispering something in her ear. Intimately. Not like an employer and his employee. More like...

They both looked at her and she stammered a bit. "Um...hey, thanks to whoever cleaned up the crickets this morning."

"Don't thank us, thank them." Jim pointed to the front door.

Through the glass she watched as first one, then

another, then another Guinea hen stuck its head around to peer inside. One pecked at the glass.

"Where did those things come from?" she asked, stifling a groan. It was way too hot to leave her car windows up all day. But now she'd have to.

"I brought them from my brother's place," Jim said. "I thought we'd conduct a little experiment and see if they don't help alleviate our cricket mess."

"I told him they'd just create another kind of mess," Carlene put in, "but he's such an optimist, he refused to listen to reason. They'll be gone in a week, anyway."

"Hey, Audrey, did you know Carlene here could cook?"

She shoved her purse in a desk drawer, noticing the gorgeous coffee cake on her desk. She grabbed a napkin and the knife, and dug in. "Of course I knew Carlene can cook. Where've you been?"

"Running a business, I guess." Jim cut himself another piece of cake, grabbed his coffee, found one free finger to push his glasses up on the bridge of his nose, then headed for his office. The Guineas outside cranked up in unison. "Carlene Fletcher baking a cake. Who would've thought."

Audrey observed her friend watching Jim disappear down the hall. When Carlene turned back to Audrey she rolled her eyes as usual, but her smile told an altogether different story.

"So what's the occasion?" Audrey poured a cup of coffee.

"No occasion. I just thought we needed a treat."

Audrey dumped a spoonful of creamer and two of sugar into her mug. She nodded and smirked. "Well, *whatever* the reason, thanks. I was hungry. I didn't get anything to eat this morning before I left."

"You're running late a lot these days."

"Oh, Carlene!" Audrey sank down into her chair. Alarm at the intimacy between her boss and her friend was forgotten at the memory of her own crazy life's developments. "You'll never guess who was waiting for me when I got home yesterday."

"Brent?"

Audrey shook her head. "Worse."

Carlene gasped. "Bobby?"

Audrey nodded as the panic she'd felt last night rose fresh and made her appetite wither and die. She could still feel where his fingers had dug into the flesh of her arm. She squeezed her eyes shut, still hearing Bobby's softly uttered plea to come home.

"What happened? Did he hurt you? Did you call the police?"

"He didn't hurt me. He said he wants to come home. He wants to be a 'family man' now, whatever that means. Said he's changed, and he'll quit drinking."

"So he didn't really have anything new to say."

Audrey shook her head and looked up at Carlene. Tears filled her eyes before she pressed the palms of her hands against them to cover it.

"Oh, no!" Carlene's tone hardened. "Tell me you didn't take him back."

Audrey shook her head again and reached for the box of tissues. She grabbed one and dabbed at her nose. "No. I didn't take him back."

"And you're not thinking about doing so either, are you?" It was more a command than a question.

"No. Not really."

"Not really?"

"No, I don't want him back." Audrey heard the words coming out of her mouth with an obvious lack of conviction. "Not the way things were..."

Carlene's brows shot up. "What? *Not the way things were?*"

"But if he–"

"No!" Carlene cut her off. "You listen to me. That man put you through hell. And if you take him back, it'll start all over again. He hasn't changed. He's not gonna change. He will always be just what he's always been. Same as his father was, and his good-for-nothing brother."

Audrey shook her head. "No, no. I know him, Carlene. And he's not like his father and brother. Not exactly. He hates what he is, and he could be so much better. He has the potential to be such a good man, if he could just–"

Carlene leaned over the desk, her face just inches from Audrey's. "He isn't going to change for you. As if six years of your life wasn't enough time to waste on him. In all that time, did he ever even try to change?"

"Yes!"

"No! All he ever did was talk about it, so that you'd believe he might. So you wouldn't throw him out. He didn't just abuse you, Audrey. He lied to you, time and time again. He's lying to you now."

Audrey felt a sudden deflation in her soul, like a balloon someone had blown up and then slowly let the air out of again. One deep breath, in, then out, and the last shred of hope she felt about Bobby disappeared with it. "I know," she whispered.

"Well, that's good to hear." Carlene leaned in closer. "Because you know if you take him back he'll probably kill you one of these days. You know that don't you?"

"I know." Audrey tossed her used tissue into the garbage can, conviction on the issue finally rearing up. Carlene was right. Bobby was charming, and they'd had plenty of good times together. But he was dangerous. This last year without him had been a solid year of peace. No injuries, no fear. She'd reconciled with her parents. She shook her head. "But I don't know what to do, Carlene. He broke into my house yesterday. When he left last August I changed the locks, but yesterday he was inside when I got there. It doesn't matter what I do, you know? How could I have ever been so stupid?"

"Call the police," Carlene said. "Get one of those restraining orders."

Audrey blew her nose and shook her head. A restraining order would just make him mad. Drunk and mad. "I'd probably be better off getting a shotgun."

Carlene gave a very unsophisticated snort. "At least that way, he'd have to decide if what you've got is worth what he'd have to go through to get it."

Audrey looked at her for a long moment. They burst into laughter at the same time, and Audrey reached for another tissue to dab away a few more tears.

It was easy, sitting here with Carlene's support, to speak of how she didn't want him back. But even as she heard the words escape her mouth, her mind was poring over all the possible ways she could avoid the ugly confrontation that was bound to follow police involvement. The most obvious way would be not putting up a fight at all, contradictory as it was to everything she knew she had to do. Of course, she couldn't completely rule out the shotgun idea.

"I guess maybe that would be the most reliable solution." Audrey sniffed, then grinned. "Can't you just see me with a shotgun? I'd probably hit everything *but* him."

"You can always come and stay with me for awhile," Carlene said practically. "I already have a shotgun. And I know how to use it. Trust me; Bobby Kerr wouldn't be the first snake I've hit with it."

❧

Brent kept one eye on the door as the waitress brought his burger and fries.

"You want me to go ahead and get your check ready now, or you want to wait a few more minutes?"

"Give it just a few more minutes." He'd waited alone in the booth for fifteen minutes before he decided to go ahead and order some supper. It took another ten minutes for his order to arrive and still he waited. She had enough time. He'd eat his burger and drink his iced tea, and then he'd leave.

It would be for the best, anyway. The last thing he wanted to deal with now, or ever, was his mother asking him for cash. Since he left home, the only times she ever took the initiative to contact him was for money.

When he spoke with her on the phone this afternoon she hadn't said a word about what she really wanted. She'd heard he was back in town and wanted to know how he was doing. She wanted to meet him for supper at the Prickly Pear.

There was more to her call than wanting to know how he was faring. She couldn't care less about that.

And now she was late. He released a heavy breath and signaled the waitress for the check.

His mother stood just inside the door surveying the room. Her glance passed over him twice before she finally settled questioningly on him. He nodded and raised a hand to wave.

Wanda Thomason had the look of a woman who led a hard life. She was somewhere in her late forties. But she looked at least ten years older. Her teeth were crooked and nicotine stained when she offered an unsure smile. And when she pushed her shoulder-length bleached hair out of her face he saw dark roots. It made him wonder for the thousandth time what his father must look like.

Wanda's dull, empty blue eyes and weathered skin told of a hard and loveless existence. But even despite his hostility, he could see traces of a once lovely young woman beneath the ill used surface.

"So, look at you." Her coarse voice sounded a little shaky to him. "I almost didn't recognize you."

"You *didn't* recognize me." He leaned back against the cool vinyl booth, interlocking his fingers and resting his clasped hands on the table.

Wanda laughed uncomfortably and looked down. "It's just that you look so good, baby." Her voice softened, but she still sounded nervous. "You look like a man. Last time I saw you, you were—"

"Eighteen years old. And I'm not sure you really noticed me then."

She looked down, then fished a pack of Camels and a lighter out of her purse. She took out a cigarette and stuck it in her mouth, then she offered him one. He declined the offer with a wave of his hand.

"I heard you were back in town is all. I just wanted

to see how you were gettin' along. To make sure you were all right."

How many hundreds of cigarettes must he have seen her light when he was a kid? Brent watched her now as she touched the lighter's flame to the small torch and inhaled deeply. Nothing about her had changed.

Brent sighed heavily. "Did you need something from me? Some money? Where're you staying now?"

"I'm OK. I've been stayin' with a friend of mine for about a week. I don't have a place of my own right now. I'm tryin' to get back on my feet. You know how that is."

He nodded and swallowed back an acerbic comment about how it was usually customary to start out on one's feet before one could really attempt to get back on them. "You sure you don't need some cash. Maybe pay your friend a little rent or buy some groceries or something? Here, let me buy you dinner." He slid a menu across the table.

Wanda shook her head and puffed on the cigarette. "No, baby. I'm good."

Doubtful. "Where are you working now?"

"Oh, I'm sort of in between jobs right now. I'm looking for a job waiting tables or something. I wonder if this place is hiring."

The bell on the front door jingled. Audrey stepped inside and approached the front counter. She placed an order, pulled some cash out of her wallet and paid the cashier, something the girl said making her smile. Then she sat down on an old wooden pew by the front door. She scanned the room, stopping when she noticed him. Nothing at all registered on her face as her glance slid from his mother to him.

Please, don't let her think that this is just some woman I picked up somewhere.

Something in her expression changed. He thought he saw recognition dawn, and a wave of relief swept over him when she smiled sympathetically.

"I heard you're buying a house. Someone said you're buying Vernon Denton's old place." The sound of his mother's voice dragged him back to the conversation at hand.

Brent nodded. "We're supposed to close tomorrow."

She cleared her throat and coughed. "That's a nice, big place."

He shrugged. "It could use some work."

"You gonna fix it up?"

"Thought I might."

His mother took a long drag from her cigarette and blew the smoke back out in a steady stream. "I could help you."

Brent narrowed his eyes. "What?"

"I could help you fix that place up. I can clean, paint, you name it. You could just tell me what you want done, and I can do it."

He pressed further back into his seat. *Here it comes.* "In exchange for what?"

She shrugged. "I don't know. Maybe I could stay with you for a while. Just 'til I get myself together, you know, and get a job and a place of my own."

Brent looked down at his hands and picked at a callus on his palm.

"I've never lived in a real house before," she said.

"Yeah? Me neither." Brent glanced back to the pew where Audrey sat. All he wanted was a glimpse of her soft blonde hair, her pretty face, her smooth skin. Just a glimpse of the future he'd wanted for years. But she was gone.

He turned his attention back to the woman who was his mother, sitting across from him with her hard features, rough hands, and bad breath. All he could think about when he looked at her was the past he wanted so desperately to forget.

"Hey, remember the last time we talked?" she asked. "When you told me you'd gotten saved?"

Brent nodded and looked down at the table.

"How's that goin'? I mean, how's God doing these days?"

He cast a sharp glance at her. "Are you trying to be funny?"

Her smile faded. "No. No. I wanna know. Whatever happened with that?"

"Nothing's changed."

She nodded and he let the subject drop. He should probably be more open to the idea of discussing his faith with her. No one he knew needed to experience a conversion more. But it was a joke to her.

"So how about it, hon?" she said finally. "You think you could let your old Mom crash with you for a while?"

Brent expelled a heavy breath and rubbed the back of his neck. "I don't know. I'll give it some thought. Call me at work tomorrow afternoon. The deal should be closed by then, and I'll let you know."

His mother smiled big as she crushed out her cigarette in the red plastic ashtray. "Thanks, baby. I promise I'll be a big help to you. I'll talk to you tomorrow."

8

Audrey switched on the coffee pot, cast a glance down the hall towards the bathroom door, then sat down and turned on her computer. Carlene had been in there since Audrey arrived fifteen minutes ago, and this after calling in sick the previous two days.

The door opened and Carlene stepped out, pressed a hand to her stomach, then closed her eyes and took a deep breath.

"Carlene?"

She leaned against the wall and pressed her lips together as color drained from her face.

"Oh my word, Carlene." Audrey stepped around the desk. "You look awful."

"I just need to freshen up my lipstick." Carlene managed a feeble smile, pushed away from the wall, and walked slowly to her office.

"No," Audrey followed. "You look sick. What is this, day three?"

Carlene sank slowly into her chair as if every little movement hurt.

"You should see a doctor. A stomach virus should have passed by now."

Her friend's miserable laugh alarmed her. "I'm not sick, Audrey."

"Not sick..?" That was crazy talk.

Carlene looked sick as a dog, with a sheen of

perspiration covering her face. She'd obviously just thrown up.

Audrey furrowed her brows. *Unless...*confusion cleared into perfect understanding on a long, slow gasp.

Carlene leaned forward, propping elbows on her desk and burying her face in her hands. "I know!" She groaned. "I know what you're thinking."

"What am I thinking?"

"That I'm some kind of loose, trashy woman."

"Why would I think such a thing?"

"You know, you being such a good Christian woman from such a good Christian family and all."

Audrey took a step back, stunned by Carlene's sarcasm. If anyone knew the error of those words it would be Carlene. Carlene might not be aware of her past with Brent, but she knew well and good how she had lived with Bobby. Not like the *good Christian woman* she should have been. She swallowed and cleared her throat. "You know as well as I do that I've done my share of wrong."

"I'm sorry, Audrey. I didn't mean it to sound like that. You're my best friend...I don't know what's wrong with me. It's like I have PMS times a hundred and I just can't..." Her voice trailed off on an unexpected sob. She covered her face with one hand.

Audrey went to her.

Carlene leaned into the embrace and cried on her shoulder until the tears abated.

"I feel like I'm in high school all over again. I know everyone thought the worst of me back then. Most of the rumors weren't even true. But now it's like they were all justified. This is how everyone thought I'd end up, and now I have..." Carlene managed to sit up and take a deep breath, sniffing as Audrey handed her a tissue.

"Oh, Carlene." Audrey's voice sounded soft and tremulous in the wake of a sudden wave of guilt. How many of those rumors had she repeated? Her behavior back then must have caused Carlene much pain. No wonder she'd lashed out sarcastically. "I'm sorry I judged you. I was stupid and arrogant, and I've never been any better than you or anyone else, even though I thought I was." She stopped and swallowed down the ache in her throat, completely humbled. "Whatever happens, you know I'm your friend, right?"

"I know." Carlene nearly sobbed again but managed to contain it. "I'm sorry. I'm just still so shocked. I took four pregnancy tests, hoping one would be negative."

"Does Jim know?" Audrey lowered her voice. She didn't know why. Jim hadn't yet arrived for work.

Every defense went up and Carlene lifted her chin belligerently. "Why should Jim need to know?"

Audrey snorted, totally unoffended by her reaction. "Well, besides the fact that he's your boss, isn't he the father?"

All the fight drained out as she leaned forward and buried her face in her hands again. "What am I gonna do? His dad is a preacher! What's he gonna think of me?"

"I guess he can't think any worse of you than he will of Jim."

Carlene sat up and dropped her hands. "I hadn't thought of that."

But then the bell on the front door jingled. Jim was here, and Carlene's recovering color drained away again.

"The first thing you need to do is tell him." Audrey whispered.

A second later Jim poked his head in her door. "Carlene? You okay?" He stepped inside as Audrey slipped past him and closed the door on her way out.

❧❧

The weekend had been blissfully uneventful. Audrey adjusted a vent in yet another vain attempt to cool down. The drive home from her office was short, but miserable with an AC that did nothing but blow more hot air around.

Today had been tranquil for a Monday. Even Gertie cooperated when the time came for her to alight from the hood of the car. The thought of the barrel shaped little Pygmy goat *alighting* from anything made her smile. But the sight of Bobby's big black four by four waiting in front of her house when she pulled into the driveway chased away the comical image. Her mirth died.

Bobby sat perched on her front porch sipping a Coke instead of a beer. And her yard looked great. It had been cut, edged, and a sprinkler was running now. The shrubs had been neatly trimmed, her little flowerbed had been weeded and watered. Even the front porch looked better. All the trash and clutter was gone. It had been swept and the little table and chairs cleaned and arranged neatly. Just outside the door sat a five-gallon bucket, paintbrushes, rollers and pans, all unused.

Audrey's heart dropped a little as Bobby stood up and smiled.

Well, she knew he'd be back.

"Hi, baby," he said. "So, how was work today?"

"Did you do all this?"

He nodded.

Apparently, after his long day of yard work he'd showered and changed. Audrey could smell his cologne from where she stood about five feet away, and it stirred a host of memories, some very bad, but some...most...good.

"You didn't have to–"

"I wanted to do something for you, Audrey. It looks like it's been awhile since the yard was cut, so I thought I could start there. I've been working for a landscaping company this past year." He grinned. "I learned a lot. And I know you haven't had anyone to take care of that since I've been gone."

"And the paint?"

"Last time I was here I noticed that you'd never had those walls repainted after I patched them. I thought I could do that for you, too."

Bobby pulled something out of his shirt pocket and handed it to her. She stepped close enough to take it from him. It was a selection of color samples from the hardware store. One of the colors was circled in red.

"Is the color OK?" Bobby asked, stepping down off the porch. "I think I spent an hour looking through all the samples. But I thought this one looked like what you would pick."

"Bobby, you shouldn't have bought all this stuff."

He looked back at the pile of painting paraphernalia and shrugged. "I can take it back if you want me to. Hal at the hardware store said that if you didn't like the color I could bring it back and trade it for another."

Audrey shook her head and gritted her teeth. That wasn't what she meant and he knew it. "It isn't that. I like the color." In fact, the color was exactly what she would have picked. "But I can't...I can't take you back."

"You don't have to take me back, not today, not ever if you don't want to." His voice turned soft. "But at least give me the chance to make it all up to you, to fix what I..." He stopped abruptly and swallowed hard. "Look, I'll do all the work during the day while you're at the office. When five o'clock comes I'll pack up and go on back to Mama's house, and I'll finish the next day if I have to."

Audrey looked down. "You're staying at your mom's?" The thought of him at that place turned her stomach. And he hated it there, too. In all their years together he'd worked hard to avoid it. She could still picture his mother, hiding in the kitchen, sitting at the table sipping coffee or iced tea. She stayed out of the way of his father, who probably hadn't laid a hand on her in years, anyway, because he was always nearly comatose in his recliner from drinking constantly.

His brother, Tommy, would be there regularly, spewing his hatred everywhere, and Tommy's delinquent children would be running roughshod over their grandmother and everyone else. She suppressed a shudder.

"Please, baby, let me do this for you. I want to do this for you." Bobby's earnest plea made the images vanish like smoke.

In the midst of a cleaning frenzy this weekend she had thought about how much she'd love to have her living room repainted, and here he was offering to do it. And it was the least he could do. After all, he was the one who'd put the holes in the walls in the first place. She gritted her teeth again, harder. How did he know just what to do and say? It was like he could read her mind. But she wasn't so foolish as to believe that he wouldn't want anything from her in exchange.

She shook her head. "You need to take all this stuff back, Bobby."

"Audrey," he said softly, smoothly, "just give me a chance to prove to you how serious I am. All those years we spent together, doesn't that mean something? Don't you know that I love you? I'd have never left if you hadn't thrown me out.

"I know I'm not the perfect man. I haven't even been a good man." He paused as the muscles in his jaw worked against the emotion he was trying so hard to control. "But I'm trying so hard to change, and I love you, and I've been missin' you, baby."

He knew her so well. He knew that every sweet word he said would wear down her resolve just a little more, would bolster her hope that the years she'd spent with him had not been a total waste. What's more, he was right.

He never had left her, and if she hadn't insisted he leave, he probably never would have. And in his own screwed-up way, he did love her. Unlike Brent had done.

But when the thought of Brent came to her now, she closed her eyes and saw his face, and she knew in her still broken heart that he was the one she wanted. Unfortunately, Bobby was who she had, who she deserved.

She finally nodded. "OK. But you have to be gone by five every day. And I'm not fixing you supper. And if you break any of your own rules, I'm calling the police."

"Deal." Relief and joy lit his expression, and he didn't even try to check it. He looked like a little boy who'd just gotten the one thing he wanted most. She felt her expression soften. "Now, how about you go down to the hardware store with me and pick out a trim color."

"OK." Her assent sounded reluctant even to her own ears. "But we'll take separate cars."

He nodded, but looked disappointed. "That'd be fine. Maybe afterwards we can go get somethin' to eat. That way you don't have to fix anything for yourself tonight."

Audrey smiled and shook her head. "No."

He nodded again, clearly on his very best behavior. He wanted a chance to win her back. And Audrey knew both of them well enough to know that, if she wasn't very careful, he just might succeed in wrangling himself another chance.

In fact, it seemed he already had.

9

How many shades of white could there possibly be?

Brent had hoped to make a quick decision, buy paint in a most basic shade; white, and get back home to continue the cleanup of his new house. Now he stood in front of the colors display trying to figure out the difference between cool white, warm white and something called "Snow White." The confusing thing was that, the more he considered all his options, the more he liked one called "Desert Taupe." He held the color sample at arm's length and turned it from side to side. What color was it exactly? Sort of brown, sort of gray. Almost a little bit reddish. Mostly brown.

Maybe he'd just get some incarnation of white for the kitchen, and this "Desert Taupe" or whatever it was for the rest of the downstairs. He'd worry about the upstairs later.

The air stirred beside him, mingling suddenly with a delicate perfume. He turned to find Audrey standing beside him also examining the white color samples.

He almost started. "Oh, hi."

"Hi." Her voice was very soft and her smile, very warm. "I take it you got the deal closed on your house without any trouble?"

He nodded. "We're going to stay at the hotel for

another week or so, until we get the floors refinished and the walls painted. At least downstairs."

Her brow furrowed. "We?"

"Oh yeah," he added quickly. "I guess you saw me with my mother the other night at the diner?"

Audrey nodded.

"She doesn't have a place right now so I agreed to let her stay at the house with me until she could find a job and a place of her own." He looked down at the samples in his hands. "She told me she'd been staying with a friend of hers, but when she found out it might be another week before I was ready to move into the house she admitted she was really living in her car."

"So you're putting her up in a hotel room?"

He shrugged and nodded. "I couldn't let her sleep in her car."

Audrey met his eyes and smiled like she was proud of him. Like *she* was proud of *him*. His heart soared.

"Is she here?" Audrey looked around. "It's been awhile, I should say 'hi' or something."

"No. I left her back at the house. She offered to help clean, so that's what she's doing."

"So, you think you can be ready to move in a week?"

He shrugged. "I don't know. I guess it all depends on what the walls look like underneath all that old wallpaper. If I have to replace any dry wall it could take longer. Your Dad offered to help out."

Small talk. That's all it was. In the manner of "how've you been?" "What have you been up to lately?" "Long time no see." But it was a far cry from that blistering afternoon a month ago when he'd first seen her again and she'd come right out and said she didn't even want to see him around. He grinned. He couldn't stifle it. For all her declarations, she still stood two feet away asking questions, prolonging their time here together.

She could deny it all she wanted. But she still had feelings for him. There was a softness in her eyes as her gaze studied his face, lingering just a little on his mouth. A woman didn't look that way at just anyone.

Finally she looked down and nodded. "Dad's good at that sort of stuff. He was his own contractor on that house of theirs, and he did a lot of the work himself. Is this your color?" She took the "Desert Taupe" sample from him and studied it.

"Yeah." He raised one hand to rub the back of his neck as he looked down, trying to cover an odd wave of embarrassment. "I...I don't know. I'm just thinking about it. There's so many to choose from. I was just gonna buy white. Never realized there were so many *shades* of white."

"I like it," Audrey said. "It's warm and masculine. It's a good color for a man's house. The outside can be white. The inside should have some color."

"And yet you're looking at the white samples." Brent grinned and took a sample from her hand.

She smiled back. "I'm picking out a trim color. It's OK if the trim is white, as long as the walls have some color."

"Oh, I see."

Audrey nodded and handed him his color. "It's really quite simple."

"Audrey, I–"

"Did you pick a color, baby?"

Brent almost jumped at the invasive masculine voice and turned to find Bobby standing a few feet away holding a roll of painter's tape in one hand and two cans of spray primer in the other.

"Yeah." Audrey's voice turned soft again. But not in that sweet, charming, feminine way she'd had with him just a few moments ago. Now she seemed timid as she handed Bobby the color sample, refusing to make eye contact with anyone.

Bobby looked at the color for a moment then turned his attention back to her, nodded, and smiled. "I almost picked this one." Brent caught the pointed glance Bobby cast his way before looking back at her. "See how well I know you. I'll go get this mixed up for us."

Brent watched Bobby walk to the end of the aisle and hand the sample to the woman behind the counter, before he looked back at Audrey, who wouldn't meet his eyes. "What's that all about?"

Audrey shrugged as if it was no big deal. "He's painting my living room for me."

Brent's jaw nearly dropped. "What about the other night when you threatened to call the police to come haul him off?" He tried to keep his voice down, but his words came out sounding like a very loud, very angry whisper.

He glanced at the counter to find Bobby watching them. Brent backed away a pace and tried hard to look nonchalant. The last thing he wanted was to stir up Bobby's temper and then send her home with it. "You're not gonna let him move back in with you, are you?"

Audrey looked shocked. "How did you know —"

"Come on, Audrey. It's no big secret."

Brent was a little surprised when she snapped at him, though she too kept her voice down.

"No, I'm not letting him move back in. He's painting my living room. He offered to do the work while I was at the office, and he promised to be gone by the time I got home. Is that OK with you? Because Heaven forbid I should do something that *you* don't approve of."

"*I'll* paint your living room if that's what you want, Audrey. I'll paint your whole house." Brent could hear the tender urgency in his voice as he struggled to keep his volume down. He fought hard against the urge to reach out and touch her. "Let me do it. I'd probably do a better job, anyway."

She softened, sighed, and finally smiled. Her eyes glistened. "It's not that simple."

Brent wanted to pull her close and pour his heart out. He'd tell her it was that simple. She only had to say the word, and he'd make sure Bobby never came around again. He'd take care of her. He stood looking down at his boots saying nothing, but his heart was pleading for her to choose him.

"I have to go." The words conveyed a finality that made his heart sink. In the space of about five minutes, he'd gone from feeling like maybe he had a shot with her after all, to realizing that, in some twisted way, she was still with Bobby.

"Audrey, wait." He followed her glance to Bobby, who was just retrieving his gallon of paint from the clerk. "He hasn't changed."

"But he's trying so hard," she whispered. "Maybe he can. Maybe he will. Like you did."

Brent watched her walk away to join Bobby at the checkout counter where he paid for the purchase. As the two were leaving the store, Bobby pressed his hand to the small of Audrey's back and whispered something in her ear. She glanced up at him, a surprised smile lighting her face at whatever he'd just said. Bobby's expression softened at her smile. He obviously loved her, as hard a fact as that was to reconcile with the way he had treated her.

Brent sighed heavily. As much as he wanted to read fear and timidity in her reaction to Bobby, he couldn't. Clearly, she felt comfortable with him, at least in this moment. The history between them showed and her life with Bobby obviously hadn't been all bad. And despite her assertion that she wouldn't take him back, the two were the picture of familiar intimacy.

He couldn't decide which he wanted more: to let her seal her own fate since she couldn't recognize that he was clearly the better man, or to run after them and beat Bobby to a pulp for every cruel thing he'd ever done to her.

Lord? He hung his head. *Is this why you brought me back here? To cause her to hope that Bobby will change in the same way I have?* He could only hope that God would intervene. All he could do was pray that if Audrey chose Bobby, the Lord would save and transform him too.

"Lord, let it be so."

෨෴

It had taken Bobby the whole week to get her living room painted.

In his defense, ironic though it was to defend him, he had started a new job at the feed store two days after their conversation about his doing the painting. His shift didn't start until ten o'clock in the morning, so he'd get up and spend two hours at her house painting, then he'd head off to his new job. But he'd been true to his word. He got the work done, and he was never there when she got home.

Her living room looked great. It didn't seem like the same room. Where once the walls had been an old yellowing ivory, now they were a calm and cool blue-gray. Even when Audrey ran her hand over the repairs, she could detect no sign of their presence. All the trim had been painted the glossy white she had chosen at the hardware store, and Bobby had even gone to the extra trouble to install and paint new crown molding around the room's perimeter.

Audrey dropped to her knees in one corner of the room and gave the carpet an experimental tug. It didn't budge so she worked the claw end of a hammer underneath the edge and started to pry. Finally the carpet gave and she pulled it back to see what the floor underneath looked like.

"I knew it!" Her excited whisper bounced off the still bare walls. She peeled the carpet back further to reveal a warm golden hardwood floor. "I knew it!"

Bobby would be all too happy to help her rip out this old carpet. They could sand and refinish it if necessary. She could get her mom to help make new curtains. There was no way she could afford new furniture, but she might be able to manage some slipcovers.

The sound of a truck door slamming jerked her out of the little dream world and fully back to reality. Bobby was here.

She'd been impressed with his keeping of his word and not coming around after she'd come home. But naturally he'd want to see her reaction to his work, so she determined to let him come in for a few minutes so she could thank him and tell him how much she truly liked what he'd done. But then she'd ask him to leave. He'd done enough for her. She wouldn't ask him to help her with the carpet. She couldn't.

A knock sounded on her front door.

Her pulse increased until she could feel her heart pounding in her chest. He might not leave peacefully just because she asked him to. She was not yet familiar enough with the new Bobby to trust that he wouldn't revert directly back to his old self if provoked.

Audrey reached for the doorknob and paused. She closed her eyes and took a deep breath.

She'd done it again. She'd let him work his way back into her life.

Suddenly it felt as if something was squeezing the air out of her lungs. It took a few seconds for her to catch her breath. The utterly trapped feeling she knew so well closed in all around her.

A second knock sounded at the door, and she struggled to compose herself. Another few seconds of breathing deeply and slowly, and she was ready. But still she had no idea what she would do.

She opened the door.

Brent stood on her front porch. Relief swept through her from her toes up, ending in a wide smile that broke out before she could stop it.

He smiled back. "Hi." Then his brow furrowed. "Everything OK?"

She could tell by his expression that he'd seen the panic when she'd pulled the door open, and her relief at the discovery that it was him and not someone else. Audrey pushed the screen door open, allowing him to come inside. "What brings you here?"

"Just passing by."

He wasn't smug, although he had every reason to be. His conclusion at the hardware store had been right. Bobby's trap had ensnared her again. And the fact that he'd been right irritated so intensely that she gritted her teeth.

"To make sure Bobby hadn't worked his way back into my bedroom?" She closed the door behind him, regretting the words the instant they came out.

Brent looked down. "No. Actually, I wanted to make sure you weren't lying incapacitated on the floor. Maybe bleeding to death with a fractured skull or a broken neck."

Now she looked down, an ache rising in her throat that brought the sting of tears with it. "Well, thanks for stopping by." She pulled the front door open again.

"Oh now, come on, Audrey. I'm sorry."

She looked at him for a long moment trying to figure out what exactly it was about him that irritated her so completely. Finally she closed the door again. "So, was there something you needed?"

"No. I just wanted to see you."

"Well, here I am." She sat down in one of her tattered armchairs as he took the sofa. "Alive and well."

"And your living room is freshly painted, I see. Looks good."

"It does, doesn't it? You can't even see where the patches were."

He nodded and looked around. "Just like they never existed."

Pressure built instantly as she clenched her teeth. "How's *your* house coming?"

"Good." He leaned forward, elbows on his knees, and hands clasped together. "We're all moved in. My mother is sleeping on the hide-a-bed in the living room for now. We're gonna start fixing up the upstairs this weekend. Next week I'm getting a bid on a new roof."

"A new roof." She winced a little. "That's going to be expensive."

"What can I do? I gotta have a roof."

She nodded and finally smiled, letting the tension go. A shaft of late afternoon sunlight filtered in from somewhere making the fair stubble on his chin glisten. She wanted to reach out and touch a fingertip to it. Suddenly the memory of how much she'd loved him as a girl arose with such clarity it hurt.

She blinked and looked away. "Do you want something to drink? I have iced tea."

"Yes." He nodded. "Thanks."

"So, how did your color come out?" She asked on the way to the kitchen. "The Desert Taupe?" She pulled a glass down and filled it with ice. "Did you go with that one after all?"

"Yeah." He said from the other room. "It looks good. I wasn't sure at first. I painted one wall of the living room and thought maybe I'd made a big mistake. But Mom said I should reserve judgment until I got the whole room painted."

"She said that?" Audrey filled his glass, trying not to sound too surprised, but not believing his mom would ever use a phrase like *reserve judgment*.

"Well, not in those exact words."

She returned to the living room to find him making a close examination of the patched wall, smoothing his hand over one spot.

"But she was right." He turned and accepted the glass of tea. "After we got the whole room painted it looked a lot better."

He held her gaze for a long moment. The concern she saw etched in his face twisted her heart until she wanted to cry. If only things could have been different between them. If she hadn't crossed that line with him all those years ago and sent herself into a tailspin that lasted for so many years. Things might have been able to develop so differently between them now. Maybe they still could.

"It breaks my heart," he began softly, "the thought of you here at the mercy of a man like him. You deserve so much better."

Do I? She wanted to ask the question only to hear an encouraging answer. Just to hear someone say she did deserve better. That life might still have all the potential she once thought it did. But the pity in his expression held her back. If he did have feelings for her, she didn't want pity to be one of them.

"You make it sound so bad." She looked away, unable to meet his gaze for a moment longer.

"You mean it wasn't?"

"Bobby's a really physical guy. He just...you and Carlene and my folks, you all make him out to be plain evil, but he's not. He just can't..." She ended on a sigh, unable to excuse Bobby this time.

Brent nodded again, but she could tell he didn't believe her. She didn't blame him. She was lying. A few times it was much worse than a few slaps and shoves.

It started out that way, but the more Bobby drank the more the violence escalated. The last time he beat her, all she'd done was ask him to turn the volume on the television down while she made a phone call. It amazed her how he could sit on the sofa, drinking all afternoon, and still come up out of his seat and punch her with the precision of a sober prizefighter. Then he grabbed the cordless receiver, ripped the phone base out of the wall and threw it at her. As if that weren't enough, he felt compelled to kick her three or four times while she cowered against a wall. Then he kicked the wall three or four times. He hadn't known she was pregnant. Not until she lost the baby later that night.

"How bad does it have to be before it's too bad?"

Mercifully, the sound of Brent's voice brought her back around to the present. "It wasn't that bad." Even she heard the waning conviction in her tone.

"Then why did Carlene tell me you were shaking at the thought of him when she talked to you about it the other day? She said you were so afraid you cried."

She crossed to the sofa and took a seat. "Carlene has a big mouth."

He laughed softly. "Well, there's not really any debating that point."

"Is this really what you came here to talk about?"

"Audrey, are you planning on letting him move back with you?"

"No. Of course not." She began to stammer. "I...I don't...I don't know. I didn't *plan* on letting him move in here the first time."

"It just sort of happened." The statement wasn't accusatory or sarcastic. It sounded more like he understood completely. "Audrey." He paused and took a breath. "I know that you spent a lot of time praying for me when we were kids. But I can't help but sense that everything is not OK with you and God."

A short, shocked laugh slipped out before she could stop it. The tables had certainly turned between them.

"Why would God bother with me now?"

❧❧

This would be Brent's second night in his new home. He shifted his truck into park and cut off the engine. The evening sky was turning dusky as the sun prepared to set, and he cast an unseeing glance at it as he climbed the steps to the kitchen door.

He heaved a weary sigh. He'd probably come on too strong, been too preachy. He'd probably gone about it all wrong and made Audrey close her heart to him again when all he really wanted to do was help.

He realized after he returned home that something major was amiss in her life. He hadn't been able to discern what it was until the night he'd stood on her front porch and confessed his faith to her. At that point he realized that she had grown cold toward God. But tonight he'd been surprised to discover the extent of her cynicism.

He pushed the door open and stepped into his dimly lit kitchen. It wasn't that she didn't believe in God anymore. It was more like she didn't really trust Him. But it wasn't even that really. He couldn't completely define her attitude, mostly because she refused to discuss it. But she'd listened to him anyway, and even thanked him for coming to visit as he left.

Brent tossed his keys onto the counter as he shut the door. He opened the refrigerator to find that his mother had taken the cash he'd given her earlier and visited the grocery store. But apparently that wasn't her only stop today. A case of beer sat on the middle shelf, already open, with a few missing. And the house smelled like smoke. New paint and cigarette smoke.

He sighed wearily, his fingers itching to grab a

beer. The longer he stood there staring at the case the closer he came to reaching in and taking one. He reached out and touched one, then balled his hand into a fist and drew it back, feeling a stirring inside him, like a warm whisper, that had, until quite recently, been blessedly familiar in guiding his decisions. Now it quietly reminded him of that moment years ago when he quit drinking. An image of that drunk cowboy and his companion in the parking lot of a bar came clearly, as did the face of the stranger who read his mind. Then came the memory of the halogen lights in the Texaco parking lot just a couple of weeks ago. He'd won this battle then, and he could do it now.

Brent took a deep breath and closed his eyes. If he lost this struggle once it would be that much easier to lose it again the next time and the next, until he quit struggling altogether and began bringing home cases of beer and liquor.

He could lose yet another job, this house, and everything. Relying on his own meager strength could quickly leave him destitute and living out of his car as his mother had been, spending what little money he could acquire on alcohol and cigarettes, and worse.

"Lord, help me," he whispered, shutting the refrigerator and rubbing the back of his neck. He went to the living room where he found his mother doing exactly what he had, just seconds ago, envisioned had he followed through with his urge.

She sat camped on the hide-a-bed, staring at the television, and holding both a beer and a cigarette in the same hand.

"Hey, darlin'." The coarseness of her voice and that phrase brought a fresh and unwelcome host of memories from his childhood. "Where've you been?"

Brent crossed the room, picked up the bowl she'd been using as an ashtray and snatched the cigarette just as she raised it to her mouth. "I'd rather you didn't smoke inside the house."

His mother blinked at him momentarily, then she drained the beer can. "I guess I'm not supposed to be drinkin' inside the house, either."

"That's correct." Brent took her empty can and carried it and the makeshift ashtray back to the kitchen. "Those are the rules."

"The rules?" His mother was up and after him in a second.

"Yes. The rules." He turned to find her glaring at him, arms folded against her chest and clad only in a t-shirt that covered her to mid-thigh. "Like curfew is at ten o'clock, or finish your homework before you go out to play with your friends, or you don't get dessert if you don't eat your dinner. Rule three in this house, by the way, is you have to wear pants in the living room and kitchen."

"Maybe you haven't noticed," she shot back caustically, "but the living room happens to also be my bedroom. You tellin' me that I have to sleep fully dressed?"

"You know what?" His temper began rising very quickly, as did his voice. "As soon as we get the roof replaced we'll fix you up a room upstairs and you can wear whatever you like. Unless, of course, you find a job and a place of your own by then." He heard himself yelling, but he couldn't stop. "Until then keep your pants on!"

"Who do you think you are, tellin' me what I have to wear and where I have to smoke and drink?" She stalked out of the kitchen.

He crushed out her cigarette and then dumped the whole contents of the bowl into the garbage.

"I'm your mother! Remember?" She returned to the kitchen wearing her jeans and carrying her half-empty pack of cigarettes and a lighter.

"Yeah. I remember. It's funny how you're choosing now to bring that up."

Wanda narrowed her eyes, and he thought for a second she might fly across the room and slap him. "Maybe I should've never come back here," she said at last. "Maybe I should leave and let you just get on with your fine new life."

"And go back to where?" He managed to get his tone of voice back under control. "Sleeping in your car?"

She stormed to the back door.

"Where you goin' now?" he asked as she yanked the door open.

"Outside to have a cigarette." She slammed the door as his cell phone began to ring.

What now?

"Hello?" He snapped the greeting into the phone.

"Brent, buddy? Is that you?"

He recognized the voice instantly—Pete Daly, his pastor and friend from College Station—and his tension slowly began to dissipate. He clutched the phone, close to a frustrated meltdown before he even realized it. "Hey, Pete."

"I didn't get your message until just a few minutes ago or I would have called back last night. How's your new life out there in the middle of nowhere?"

"Not too great at the moment."

10

An ominous line of smoke billowed and curled toward the sky. Audrey stepped out of her car and peered down the road in the direction of the highway that led past her folks' house and clinic. Intuition told her something was wrong, even before she heard Jim's anxious voice.

"Audrey!"

She turned to see him coming toward her at a jog. The town's fire alarm sounded, calling all volunteer firemen to duty.

"Your mother just called. She couldn't get you on your cell phone. There's a fire at their place. They need you out there now."

A fire? At their place? Her brain refused to process the information.

"I think it's urgent, Audrey." He touched her shoulder, breaking the spell of disbelief. "Go, now. Carlene and I are right behind you."

The five minute drive from her office to the clinic seemed so much longer. And the stream of questions flowing through her mind felt like torture. What was on fire? Grass? The house? The clinic? Was everyone OK? Why had her mother called and not her father? Was he injured, or worse?

Each yard felt like a mile, until finally her parents' property came into view. Smoke rolled off the ground, making it difficult to see exactly what the damage was so far, but as she inched closer, pulling into the gravel drive that would lead to the parking lot of the clinic, her chest constricted, and tears, hot as any fire, blurred her view.

Blazing orange flames already completely engulfed the shed out back, sending glowing embers up into the wind toward the house where another grass fire had ignited. Flames rolled up the privacy fence and onto a trellis, heavy with climbing roses, that scaled the height of the house. Right up to the roof.

"Oh Lord, no." The whispered phrase emanated from her like a last breath. "No."

She threw the gear shift into park and ran from the car, past the clinic to join her mother.

She pressed one hand to her mouth as she struggled to fully comprehend the image in front of her. It was real. It had to be. She was standing here looking at it, breathing in the suffocating smoke, feeling the heat of the flames even from all these yards away.

Audrey dropped to her knees beside her mom, who sat sobbing, cross-legged on the dry grass with her purse clutched to her chest and her phone in hand. She put one arm around her mom's shoulders and opened her mouth to speak, but no words formed.

The sound of heavy machinery starting up behind them only vaguely registered, and she turned around, letting her blurry gaze survey the action closer to the clinic. A neighbor had brought a backhoe and was digging a wide trench around it. Audrey swallowed hard and then choked on smoke. Her mind knew that the break would help prevent the flames from encroaching on that land, but her heart had already given up hope. The way the wind was blowing this morning, they'd probably lose everything.

Her dad's pickup, filled with things from within the house, sat parked next to the clinic. Brent's pickup was backed right up against the porch of the house. It was nearly full already. But it was too late.

Audrey swiped at the tears which now flowed freely. It took every ounce of restraint she possessed to keep from breaking into sobs like her mother. A handful of volunteer fire fighters surrounded the house, but with no access to a hydrant, and armed with only small water tanks on their backs, they could do little more than try to keep the fire from spreading. A sudden gust of wind buffeted them, as if in derision, and kicked up smoldering embers, carrying them away.

She rose and started for the house, but her mom grabbed her hand and held her back with a sob. "It's too late."

"Are Daddy and Brent inside?" Audrey tried to sound calm, but failed miserably. She cringed at the panicked sound of her voice, and took a deep breath. Her distress would help nothing.

Her mom nodded. "We were trying to get as much out as we could. It really looked like everything would be OK. Five minutes ago they had it all under control. But then the wind picked up and the roof caught fire. Now look!" A fresh batch of sobs tore through her. "The whole second story is burning!"

Lyndon and Brent emerged through the front door along with billowy black smoke. Both men coughed as they carried armfuls of the Rhodes' belongings and dumped them into the bed of the truck. Brent turned to make another trip into the house, but Lyndon called to him. Audrey felt her mother's grip on her hand tighten, and she tightened her own in return. Lyndon shook his head, obviously trying to convince Brent that they'd done all they could. Brent argued and turned to go back again, but this time Lyndon grabbed him by the arm.

Audrey squinted, trying to see them through the thickening smoke, her heart pounding harder with every wave of smoke that obstructed her view. All she could see were the flailing arms of the men on the front porch as they continued to discuss the situation. Every so often she'd catch a piece of their conversation, the sound of their raised voices, carried by the wind. Then both men lunged from the porch and ran for Brent's pickup. A split second later she heard the popping and cracking of the rafters as the roof collapsed onto the second story. It felt like her heart dropped along with it. Within moments the house would be a total loss. By this afternoon it would probably be gone.

Brent and Lyndon got into the truck and Brent drove it to safety within the space the trench would protect when finished.

Audrey hadn't even realized that her mother stood and now clung to her, sobs racking her body as she watched her home burning to the ground. A fresh batch of tears began to fall and she wrapped arms around her mother.

Raised voices behind them startled her, and she turned to find Brent, her dad, Carlene and Jim standing behind them.

Paula turned to Lyndon and he held her tightly. "It's OK, darlin'. We're all alive and not hurt, and we saved a few things. I got your photo albums and your jewelry box. It's gonna be OK."

Audrey looked down feeling the intense heat of the blaze at her back. The ordinarily warm morning breeze felt almost cool on her face now that she had her back to the fire. Two strong, stable hands came to rest on her shoulders from behind, and she knew without looking they were Brent's.

No one said a word, but she could feel the realization dawning on all of them that the house and everything that remained inside was a lost cause. Now they had to focus on stopping the still encroaching fire and saving the clinic.

Audrey glanced back up at her father for direction. He tenderly wiped the tears from his wife's face, his soot-laden thumbs leaving dark streaks on her fair skin. He kissed her and then handed her a shovel.

To her left, Audrey heard Jim instructing Carlene to go back to the clinic and hook up every water hose she could find and be ready to put out anything the wind blew over the trench. Then he took up his own shovel and followed her parents who had already gone to join the team of volunteer firefighters south of the house.

The house continued to burn, completely abandoned.

She wiped tears and turned to Brent whose clothes, skin and hair were covered in ash and soot. Sweat poured and he used the collar of his shirt to wipe it out of his eyes. "Should we start moving the animals? I can start loading them."

He coughed and squeezed his eyes shut for a second. "I think you better. Just in case."

Audrey nodded and looked back at the house. The sight of the collapsed roof and the flames came as a shock despite the fact that she'd watched the house burn.

"Daddy built that house. Twenty-five years ago."

Brent laid a hand on her shoulder and gave a gentle squeeze, and she tried to swallow down the scratchy, dry ache in her throat. Then he picked up the shovel he'd brought from the clinic and turned for the flames on the north side of the house.

❧⚬❦

Around six o'clock a waitress from the Prickly Pear brought paper sacks filled with cheeseburgers and fries along with gallons of water and iced tea. Audrey was famished, and she ate gratefully if silently alongside her mother and father. Every joint and muscle ached with exhaustion.

They had saved the clinic, but the remains of their home continued to smolder.

Audrey closed her eyes, took a deep breath, and let it out on a long sigh. They'd built this house the year she started kindergarten. Any memories she had of the house where they'd lived before this one were vague and disconnected from the time line of her past. Just wispy little flashes, like sitting on a green shag carpet watching Sesame Street in a darkly paneled living room, or being lifted onto the kitchen counter to watch her mom cook. *This* had been where she'd grown up.

Her upstairs corner bedroom had two windows. Out of one she could see her father's clinic and the highway in front. From the other she could look out on clear spring mornings to see a field covered with the blue and pink sheen of bluebonnets and prairie paintbrushes.

"Brent offered the use of his barn to store our things until we can get another place." Her father's voice broke the silence. "We should probably drive on out there and get it unloaded before dark."

Her mother looked at her dad with red, swollen eyes brimming once again. Her father looked completely defeated. Maybe it was the soot that had settled into every crease and wrinkle in his face. Or maybe it was the despondent sag of his shoulders, or the weariness in his voice, but suddenly he seemed so much older than he ever had before.

"Daddy, why don't y'all go on back to my house and get cleaned up and rest. Let me and Brent unload the stuff."

He shook his head, but a quiet sob from her mom drew his attention and Audrey knew he would relent. He sighed heavily, put his arm around his wife, then he nodded.

"OK." He choked on the word and turned to face the highway, staring blankly as if considering the possibility of climbing into his truck and simply driving away. But then something real seemed to command his attention.

Audrey followed his gaze to the big black four by four she had come to dread turning into the driveway and coming toward them. When Bobby stepped out, she could feel her father's energy return. It only took a second for him to come up off the tailgate, and from the corner of her eye she saw Brent approaching from the clinic.

Oh, no!

She pressed her fingertips to her eyes and rubbed hard, as if Bobby were just a figment of her imagination that she could blink away. Exhaustion had set in hours ago. All she wanted was get the trucks unloaded, go home, shower and sleep. But now an ugly confrontation was coming if she didn't do something quickly.

She stepped between Bobby and her father just as Lyndon snapped. "What are *you* doing here?"

"I just came out to check on y'all." Bobby's reply was smooth and amiable despite Lyndon's hostility. "To see if maybe there was somethin' I could do to help out. Audrey, honey, why didn't you call me?"

He'd been drinking. The stench of it layered a sense of betrayal on top of the urgency she felt to keep Bobby and her father separated. He hadn't quit after all. Everyone else was right about Bobby. He would never change.

He must have sensed her disappointment because something in his demeanor changed. She could never say what it was that told her he'd crossed his fine borderline between irritation and fury. Maybe a look in his eye, or the set of his jaw. A sudden intangible tension enveloped him and spread, spirit-like, to everyone else. For the moment he seemed pleasant enough, but underneath she knew the rage seethed.

"We could have used your help about six hours ago," her father said roughly, the defeat of moments ago edged out by anger. "But we don't need or want you here now."

She had to separate them. Whatever else happened, even if it meant leaving here with Bobby, she had to keep the two of them from coming to blows. She took Bobby by the arm and turned him back toward his truck, keeping her voice low and soft. "I think maybe you should go now."

"Why should I leave?" Bobby jerked his arm roughly away from her grasp, making sure everyone could hear him. "I was a member of this family for six years before you threw me out."

"You were *never* a part of this family!" Lyndon launched himself from where he stood apparently bent on cracking Bobby's skull with whatever strength he had left.

Brent got there in time to hold her father back. "Don't you think there's been enough trouble here for one day?" Brent's voice sounded calm and even, almost soothing. "These folks have just lost their home."

"What do you know about *these folks*?" Bobby turned on Brent. "You haven't even been back in town two months yet and suddenly you're an expert on everyone. You're nobody. Just a trailer-trash loser. Comin' back here with your fancy education making Audrey think maybe you'll stick around this time."

Audrey wrapped her arm around Bobby's and tried to urge him toward his truck. "Just go, Bobby," she pleaded softly. "We can talk about all this later."

"Just go." He mimicked her. "Or what? Or your old Daddy and your new boyfriend over there will come knock some sense into me?"

"Bobby, please..." She tugged on his arm again, urging him away.

"Let go!" He turned on her before there was time to think, shoving her away so hard it sent her crashing into the side of her father's truck. The mirror caught her in the shoulder, sending a burst of pain shooting down her arm and back.

Her cry seemed to come from somewhere outside as her mind and emotions disengaged as they had so many times before. Audrey slid down to the ground, waiting for Bobby to pull her up by the front of her shirt with one hand, then backhand her with the other. She closed her eyes and raised her arms defensively in anticipation of the blows. But they never came.

A vague, dreamlike awareness settled around her, of raised voices and violence that didn't yet involve her. She opened her eyes to find that Brent had launched himself at Bobby and was now alternately hauling, then shoving him toward his truck. There was a loud exchange of words, though she couldn't completely make them out. Something about it not being as much fun when there's someone around who'll fight back.

Bobby went down when Brent punched him. Bobby struggled back to his feet, and Brent punched him again. Audrey leaned back against the truck's tire thinking perhaps she should get up and do something. But her eyes drifted closed again. It felt indescribably good to have someone intervene on her behalf.

The sound of a siren brought her mind fully back to awareness. Her eyes snapped open. The sight, and smell, and sound of all that had gone on brought reality crashing down again. Both her mother and Carlene knelt beside her. Her father had run to join the fray happening at Bobby's truck.

"Who called the police?"

"I did." Carlene said, helping her to her feet. "As soon as he pulled in. I didn't figure he was here to help, and it's way past time someone called them."

Audrey blinked at Carlene, realization just now dawning. "Carlene, you shouldn't be here. All the smoke..."

"Hush, now." Carlene answered. "Everything's

fine."

She stood up, stretched her back and rolled her shoulder, measuring the pain. It would be fine. But nothing else would.

The siren stopped in time with the patrol car that parked beside Bobby's truck. Only one deputy had come, Justin Barnet. He'd already been out here a few times today, keeping tabs on the fire. He quickly put an end to the fight, then just as deftly began sorting out the mess between Bobby and Brent and her dad.

"Sit." Carlene ordered, pointing Audrey to the tailgate of her dad's truck.

Audrey climbed stiffly up onto it and took the cup of water her mother offered. "Mom, I'm sorry." She rubbed a hand across her forehead and down her face.

"It's not your fault, baby."

"It is." She looked at her mom miserably. "He's been back for a few weeks now."

"Living with you again?"

"No!" Audrey shook her head. "No. But he's been around. Coming to see me. Telling me he wants to come home." Judging by the look on her mom's face, it would probably be best not to mention that she'd let Bobby paint her living room and clean up her yard— that she'd pretty much placed him on a probation period with an unspoken possibility of future reconciliation.

Her mother's face turned red and she started to stammer incoherently, finally ending with a shout. "Why didn't you tell somebody?"

"She told me." Carlene offered. "And Brent."

Paula expelled a long breath, seeming to calm some at the thought that it hadn't been a secret from everyone.

Audrey looked up to see Deputy Barnet striding purposefully toward her, his face grim. She took a deep breath in and let it out slowly, hoping that doing so would clear up her perpetual confusion and bring to light the right answer to the question he was about to ask.

He stopped and looked her over. "You OK?"

She nodded. "Yes, fine."

"What happened?"

"Um..." She glanced at her mom. "He...Bobby showed up a few minutes ago. He and my dad started arguing and then Bobby shoved me. And I...um...I fell back against the truck here."

"So he argued with your father, but he assaulted you?"

"Well...yes." She got his point.

"Audrey," Justin gave her a long, serious look. "Do you want to press charges?"

Audrey bit her lip and looked around. Carlene folded arms across her chest and glared. Her mother looked at her similarly, her mouth set into a stern line. Several yards away, Brent and her father focused intensely on her as if something important hinged on her answer.

Something did.

Lord, I wish I was anywhere but here right now.

No. The word was right on the tip of her tongue. She had never pressed charges. It was so much easier just to let it go and hope it didn't happen again. But her family and friends all stood right here looking at her. They kept telling her that it would happen again, and again. And they were right.

But if she pressed charges, then what happened to her when Bobby got out of jail? He'd probably be out in a day or so. Then what? She glanced over where he sat in the back of the patrol car nursing a busted lip and a bloody nose, looking generally belligerent and hateful.

Further away was the assembly of volunteer firefighters who remained, casting curious glances in her direction as they packed up their equipment to leave. Audrey sighed and tried to swallow the scratchy ache in her throat. More than anything in the world she wanted the ground to open up and swallow her.

"Audrey? He's already going to jail tonight for DWI. I just need to know if you want to add assault to the charges against him."

Yes. The answer came on the breeze and settled into her soul. *Yes.*

No matter what happened next, "yes" was the answer she needed to give. It was the answer everyone here needed to hear. Including Bobby.

She nodded. "Yes."

Justin nodded, satisfied, then turned and strode back to his patrol car, where he stood Bobby up, turned him around and began stating his rights as he reached for his handcuffs.

"What?" Bobby's exclamation carried back. He tried to wrench his arm out of Justin's grasp.

As if that was all the resistance he needed, Justin hauled Bobby to the hood of his car and shoved him face down onto it.

"All right, all right!" She heard Bobby's acquiescence as Justin fastened the handcuffs around his wrists and pulled him back up again. Bobby glared at her as Justin pressed him into the back of the car.

She looked down and felt Carlene and her mother both crowd closer on either side.

Lord, did I do the right thing?

She held her breath waiting for an answer, hoping that God wasn't as through with her as she'd assumed all these years, because she had a feeling that within a few days she would need serious guidance, not to mention protection.

Is it too late to start doing the right thing? And if not, did I do it?

Justin got into his patrol car and pulled out of the clinic parking lot, taking Bobby to jail.

It's never too late. The still small voice replied. *And, yes, you did.*

11

"That's the last one."

Fortunately, Brent had plenty of boxes left from his move. Audrey helped him work quickly to box as much as they could of her parents' belongings to store in the barn. She tried to stretch the encroaching stiffness out, thankful that Brent insisted on taking the time to box all this stuff. The way this day had gone, she'd have been all for just tossing it in a pile and leaving it for later. But this way was better.

A roll of her neck and shoulders dragged a soft groan from her. The tenderness from her impact with the truck was worse than she thought it would be. Or maybe she'd just grown softer in the year since Bobby left.

"You OK?"

It was the first time Brent addressed her with anything other than a direction or suggestion regarding their task.

Audrey nodded. "Yes. Fine."

"I mean your shoulder."

She let out a weary sigh. "I ache all over, same as you probably do. The shoulder is nothing."

He handed her the corner of a blue plastic tarp. "It's not nothing."

They pulled the tarp open and settled it down over the surprisingly small stack they'd made against one wall of the barn. Such a minuscule pile of things, and all that remained of what had once been her childhood home.

What a long and tragic day. Audrey stepped to the doorway and stood watching the very last vestiges of sunlight being gradually snuffed out by the coming night.

Brent turned off the light in the barn and came to stand beside her, letting out a long, weary breath. Silently they watched the warm amber of the summer horizon give way to the faintest trace of a light so clear it seemed to have no color. In a moment the light was gone. Brent ran a sooty hand through his hair and across his face, obviously every bit as weary as she.

He touched her elbow and guided her out of the barn. Then he turned, slid the barn door closed and bolted it shut.

They walked in silence back to the pickup trucks they'd parked a little closer to the house. On an impulse which she was too tired to stop and think about, she slipped her hand into his and breathed a little sigh when his fingers tightened around hers.

She felt comfort there, and reassurance. He had hardly spoken since they'd arrived, and she hated the thought of him angry with her. But she understood. She was angry and disgusted with herself for letting Bobby get close enough to hurt her again. When she sent him away a year ago she thought she was so strong. She had been through with him.

How she'd ever come to be living that way in the first place, she didn't even know. Like everyone else, she'd heard all the stories about women who let their boyfriends and husbands beat up on them. She'd heard all about how they had abusive fathers and horrid childhoods. But she'd had neither of those things. And before Bobby, she'd known with the righteousness that only a very naive young woman can have, that she would *never* let someone do that to her.

She had dug this hole she was in with Bobby, and now she had dragged Brent down into it with her. No. She didn't blame him for his anger.

"I'm sorry, Brent." She spoke softly when they reached her dad's truck.

"Audrey..." His voice sounded rough and pained, and before she had time to decode his tone or his expression in the dusky light, he pulled her to him and wrapped his arms around her.

Tears surged at the comfort and relief she felt there. She slid her arms around his waist and tucked her forehead into the curve of his neck, breathing in the smoky scent of his shirt and letting her eyes drift closed.

So many years she had longed for this, for him to hold her because he cared for her, though she never thought it might be possible. She still loved him so much, and today he had defended her with feeling beyond mere chivalry. He had been more than angry as he'd hauled Bobby away from her. The old Brent would never have behaved the way he did today. The old Brent couldn't have been troubled to help his neighbors try to save their property. If he had witnessed an act of domestic violence, he would have turned his head and walked away, figuring it was none of his business.

This new Brent cared what happened to others. He cared what happened to her.

"I could have killed him today, Audrey." The words, whispered intensely against her ear, sent a shiver through her. "God forgive me, but I could have beat the life right out of him when I saw him shove you. And when I realized he intended to..." He expelled a long breath and held her closer. "It's one thing to know that sort of thing happens, or even to imagine it or hear about it. But to actually *see* it happening...and to someone you love..."

Her breath caught. *Someone you love....*

Lord? Is this really happening?

"Please, Audrey," he whispered desperately. "Even if you don't want me. Please tell me you won't take him back."

Audrey reached up and cradled his face in her hands, shaking her head. "I won't."

"Promise me." His hands moved to her waist and his gaze pierced hers, pleading.

"I promise." She whispered the words then pressed her lips softly to his, once, then twice. "I promise." She whispered against them.

He responded hesitantly, but he didn't push her away. Instead he took a deep, measured breath, as if trying to decide what to do next. She let her eyelids drift closed and pressed her cheek to his, memorizing the smoky scent that still clung to his skin and clothes, feeling the rise and fall of his chest, and the stir of his breath on her skin.

"I love you, Brent." The words streamed out before she could stop them. Try as she might to board up her heart and not let him touch it again, she would never succeed. "I've always loved you. Even that day at the Prickly Pear...I knew the second I saw you that I still loved you."

A sound escaped him; half sigh, half groan, and he pulled her tightly to him as if those words were all the permission he needed. He deepened the kiss that she started with an intensity that both startled and thrilled her.

The heat from his hands radiated through the thin cotton of her blouse, instantly eradicating all rational, logical thought. His mouth was so soft and sweet. And although he had kissed her before, she had waited her whole life for him to kiss her like this.

Audrey wound her hands into the fabric of his shirt and tried to pull him closer, though no space separated them at all, and she clung, yielding completely to whatever he wanted in this moment. He loved her, and she was his.

But before she had time to say as much, his hands slid to her shoulders and he gently pressed her an arm's length away. She blinked a few times, trying to restore some measure of balance. He let go and took a couple of steps back, raising one balled fist to his mouth.

Then he turned away.

❧

Brent took several deep, measured breaths, keeping his back to her for the long moment necessary to regain the control he'd tried so hard to maintain. He'd kept a tight rein on himself since nearly losing it at the clinic and beating Bobby until he was incapable of standing upright, let alone ever hurting Audrey again.

He regretted that she probably thought he was angry with her. He wasn't. He was proud of her–proud that she finally had that good-for-nothing loser taken to jail where he belonged. But he'd been unable to speak since then, for fear his tenuous self-control would collapse, leaving his fear for her exposed for all to see.

But when she slipped her hand in his, and it had felt so small and vulnerable and trusting, something snapped and the walls began to crack. Then she kissed him and said she loved him–had always loved him, and they crumbled completely.

He took one last, long breath and turned back to face her, trembling. Literally shaking in the wake of the words they'd just exchanged.

She clamped a hand over her mouth and a tear rolled down her soot smudged cheek.

"Oh, Brent," she whispered, lowering her hand and taking a few steps backward. "I'm so sorry."

He hadn't wanted this. Not this way. He hadn't wanted to touch her or initiate this contact yet–tonight especially. After everything that happened today; the fire, the confrontation with Bobby, he hadn't wanted to confuse or take advantage of her. It seemed a bit late to worry about that now. If she was going to turn to him, he didn't want it to be out of a need for comfort alone. He wanted it to be real and right.

Yet there she stood, desperately needing comfort and reassurance, and he couldn't stand not to give it when it was within his power to do so. He reached out and moved to close the distance between them, but she put her hands up and sidestepped him, as if he were a live wire and one touch could mean death.

"No!" She responded, but not angrily. "No. You're right. I should never have...I just didn't think..." Finally she shook her head. "Here I've been the one pushing you away and telling you to leave me alone and now I...I...and tonight...we're both exhausted. I'm sorry."

She gave a frustrated groan. "Will I never learn? I am *so* stupid."

"Don't say that." He reached out and brushed her hair away from her eyes. "You're not stupid. You're right about this not being the right time. It's just not the right *time*, that's all. And the last thing I want is to do anything that might hurt you. Something that you–that we both–would regret later."

The pulsing drone of cicadas filled the silence as she stood for a long moment, seemingly at a loss for what to do or say next. Finally, she took the few steps toward her father's truck. She reached for the handle, but paused.

"Thank you, Brent," she said softly. "For everything. For helping with the fire today, and with Bobby..."

Brent looked down. "I'm sorry about your folks' house."

Audrey nodded. "Well, Daddy built that one. I guess he can build another." Her words sounded practical, but her eyes filled with tears. She sniffed and opened the door.

"You won't take him back, will you? He will never treat you like you deserve to be treated. He never has and he never will."

Her tears spilled over at his sudden entreaty.

He felt like a jerk, bringing it up again and making her cry. But he wanted to make sure she remembered her promise. It felt like minutes passed before she finally took a breath to speak again, minutes during which he thought she might renege.

"I don't want Bobby back," she whispered at last, pushing the truck door closed again. "More than anything I wish he'd just disappear into thin air. But we were together for so long..." She paused and looked down, shaking her head.

"Me and him, we sort of deserve each other. I lived with him for six years. And no matter how much I used to tell myself that I loved him, and that it was just the same as being married, it wasn't.

"But I can't undo it. He still seems to have this hold on me, and I just can't break free...and look at you. So changed, so decent. You need someone more like you. Someone more like I used to be."

"You seem to have forgotten how it is *I* used to be," he said softly.

Audrey looked down and shook her head again.

"No," she said, "I haven't forgotten."

Despite her smile, she looked quite sad. So sad. Completely defeated and disillusioned with her life. And he could remember with great clarity how that felt. As if it was yesterday. He snagged her hand, felt her tense, then relax as she allowed him to pull her closer.

"Audrey," he began softly, "you've told me what you don't want, and you've told me what you think I need. So now tell me what it is that *you want*. What do you need?"

Audrey shrugged and sighed heavily, but she remained silent for a long moment. She seemed alternately on the verge of baring her soul and giving up. Finally she looked down and took a deep breath.

"I want to be eighteen again. I want to go back and do everything over, and do it right." Her voice was soft and breathy, and he knew she was fighting hard not to cry. "I want to be happy again." She raised her tearful gaze to meet his. "I want to be rid of Bobby for good, and I want to forget that I ever knew him at all. I want..."

Her voice trailed off, but she didn't look away from him.

She was leaving so much unsaid. But it was all plain as day on her face. And he knew what she couldn't say. How much heartache could have been avoided if he had just listened to her all those years ago? Back when she'd been young and eager for the Lord to save him so they could grow up together, equally yoked. But if there was a way to go back and change things, would he? He couldn't imagine being able to say yes to God before he'd sunk as low as he had that night outside the bar when God reached down and pulled him up out of the pit.

"And if we could go back and do things differently, make different choices, do you think we would make better ones?" He leaned beside her against Lyndon's pickup. "Would you be better off now?"

She looked back down and shook her head. "I'd like to think so. I'd like to think that I wouldn't have made such a mess of my life. Or gone so far for so long in the wrong direction."

"I wonder." Brent said softly. "I know you did your best to convince me of God's love when we were kids. But I always thought that for God to love me I had to be perfect and clean to begin with. And you know as well as anyone that I was far from that. And I only got worse when I left. Oh, Audrey, I did some things..." He let his voice trail off and swallowed hard against the ache that rose in his throat at an image of another girl. A pretty girl with red hair and freckles, whose face contorted with grief and anger, and maybe even spite as she told him what she'd done.

He shook the image from his mind and swallowed again. "I was sure that I had crossed some sin-line that God couldn't or wouldn't reach beyond. It took me awhile, even after I became a Christian, to realize that God is so much bigger than that. Than me. And there was nothing I had done that could make a channel too wide for Him to reach across."

"But I was already a Christian, Brent." She shook her head despondently. "I knew better. I could have changed my direction at any time. I thought about it hundreds of times. But I just didn't. It was easier not to."

"I knew better, too, Audrey." The admission was still difficult for him. "I might not have been a Christian, but I still knew better. I still knew how I was living was wrong. And guess what. I still struggle to do what's right. That night after we went to dinner, when you told me you didn't want to see me again...I stopped by the convenience store on the way home to pick up a six pack."

Audrey looked up sharply.

"I had it on the counter. I had it paid for before I realized what the impact of what I was doing might be. And just the other night, I came home and my mother had bought a case and stuck it in the fridge. I almost took one. Boy, did I want one."

"But you didn't," she said dismally. "You *almost* made the wrong choice. But you didn't."

"But I did today. With Bobby. Did I want to knock him senseless? Yeah. Should I have? Probably not. Did I really need to? No."

"But–"

"Audrey." He had to clear away the scratchiness that rose suddenly to his throat. Whether it rose as a final product of the day's events, or at the sudden realization that she was about to totally excuse his behavior today, he couldn't tell. "Why are you so quick to forgive me my struggles–me of all people–and not your own? God made us. He knows us. He knows we're not perfect. That's the whole point of salvation. That's why He sent Christ. And I promise you, He wants you to come back to Him. Don't think about it a hundred more times. Do it now."

Audrey's eyes were open wide, and her expression was as receptive as Brent had ever seen it. Meager and obvious as they seemed, he could see her drinking in his words. She stood perfectly still, silently thinking about what he'd said, then she smiled and nodded.

Point taken.

She nodded and pulled the truck door open again. "I should go see how Mom and Dad are doing." She climbed up into the cab and put the key into the ignition.

"You'll call me if you need anything, right?"

"I will." She smiled more easily.

He nodded and closed her door.

The last time he'd told her to call had been the afternoon Bobby accosted her in her front yard. He'd known then that, even though she'd told him she would, there was no way she'd ask for his help. But this time she'd meant it.

෴

As recently as a month ago, if someone had told Audrey that Brent Thomason would be counseling her spiritually—even ministering to her—she would have shamelessly laughed out loud. But that's exactly what he had done when they'd stood together outside his barn. She had hung on his every word, hungry for the idea that God's forgiveness might yet extend to her.

She'd thought of little else since.

Brent had come to meet them at sunrise to help look for anything salvageable from the house. It only took a few minutes to determine there was nothing left. But Brent and Lyndon continued to pick here and there among the charred bricks and shattered glass.

Audrey watched him as they worked.

He'd grown up to be a decent man after all. Goodness knew these past ten years she'd had her doubts that he'd ever amount to anything other than a lecherous drunk. But instead he reached the full potential she had seen in him when they were kids. Maybe he'd even exceeded it.

He glanced up and caught her watching him. Their gazes met and locked, and then he smiled. It wasn't a sympathetic smile expressing compassion for the loss of a family home, nor was it a pure smile recalling the last conversation they had. This was the "I know what you're thinking" smile of their childhood, the same one that had launched all her emotional turmoil as a teen. It gave his face a distinctly boyish cast, and the warmth of it melted away years of waste and regret. She stood here, a girl again, with her whole life ahead of her.

He turned back to the task at hand, but not before casting one more glance her direction as if to make sure she was still watching him.

Audrey smiled to herself and turned around, running headlong into her mother.

"I take it you've forgiven him for whatever it was that went wrong between you all those years ago." Her mom smiled knowingly. "I had a feeling you might."

It was true. She hadn't thought about their one night together and his wrong behavior in weeks. Between Bobby's distraction, Carlene's predicament, and now the fire, she hadn't had time to dwell on it, and when she thought of it, she recalled only her responsibility in the matter.

Thinking about it now, the stinging humiliation of seeing him again was gone, as was her fury at being used. Somewhere in the past few weeks she'd let it go. She smiled again and nodded slowly.

"I guess I have."

Her mom obviously wasn't listening. Audrey followed her gaze to her dad, who now sat in the cab of his truck staring off into the distance.

"I'm worried about your father," her mom said. "I can't even mention cleaning this place up or what we're gonna do about a new place to live without him completely shutting down. He refuses to talk about it."

"That's his way, I guess," Audrey said, still watching her father.

"I guess." Paula sounded peeved. "I guess that's always been his way."

"Maybe he needs a few days to let the shock wear off," Audrey offered, turning back to her mother.

Paula shook her head and sighed heavily. "You know as well as I do that a few days will turn into a few weeks and then a few months. Maybe even a few years."

She wanted to argue. She wanted to persuade her mother that her father was just still in shock, and that his mood might last a few days, but then he'd snap out of it. Maybe if they both believed it, it would be true.

"He's always so good in the middle of a crisis,"

Her mom said, as if to herself. "It's after everything calms down...I hate to ask it of you, honey..." Paula turned her attention back to Audrey. "You're already doing so much by putting us up at your house. But we may need some extra help at the clinic. Brent can take care of all the medical details, and I can manage the accounts, but...I don't know. Maybe everything will be OK. Or maybe you could come out just on weekends..."

Her voice trailed off, and then she covered her mouth with her hand.

"Mom?"

Her mother shook her head and held a hand up. Then she turned abruptly and hurried back to her car.

Audrey turned to look back at her father. He was watching his wife, the bland expression on his face illustrating his complete detachment as she drove away. After her car had disappeared down the highway, he sighed and turned his attention back to the empty distance before starting his pickup and driving the short distance back to the clinic.

She shifted her glance to Brent who had apparently been watching the exchange with her mom. He smiled reassuringly. She smiled back, comforted by his presence. Then she gave him a parting wave and turned toward her car.

Though it felt much later, her day was just beginning. She had to be at work in ten minutes.

12

Brent shut the kitchen door and tossed his keys onto the counter. The increasingly familiar sound of the television greeted him and he glanced through the dining room to find his mother in her usual spot on the couch.

The stale scent of smoke lingered, mixed with a nauseatingly sweet air freshener that didn't help at all.

Brent wanted to get her moved into her room upstairs tonight. He wanted to try to get her off his couch as soon as possible. But now he wondered if giving her that much privacy might actually increase the likelihood of his home going up in flames like the Rhodes' house had a week ago. As long as he was home and she was downstairs, Wanda would take her cigarettes outside to smoke. But once she moved upstairs she'd be in a world all her own.

It looked as if he'd sleep in safety for at least one more night. When he left this morning all the room lacked was a final coat of paint, a job that probably wouldn't have taken more than a couple of hours. But if he were a betting man, he'd wager that she hadn't lifted a brush all day despite her initial promise to help out.

Last night he'd asked her to finish the painting this morning so the walls could have all day to dry. The plan had been that he would come home this evening and put together the double bed he'd bought and move the new dresser from where he'd been storing it in the bedroom next door.

He sighed, rubbed the back of his neck, and strode heavily to the living room. The sight of her camped out on the sofa bed watching some pointless talk show stoked his irritation. Three empty beer cans lay strewn on the side table. No sign of the ash tray.

"You're just in time." Wanda cleared her throat but it ended up as a cough. "They're about to tell the results of the DNA test so they'll know who the father is."

Irritation swelled into anger at her assumption that he could possibly be interested in watching a television show whose sole purpose was to mock people whose lives so clearly paralleled hers–and his, for that matter.

"You get that room upstairs painted?" His tone was harsh, but he was beyond giving her the benefit of the doubt.

"Oh, honey, I got one wall done, but then the fumes started to give me a headache so I came down for a break and some fresh air. I never did get back to it."

The irony of her needing fresh air almost made him laugh. "You never did get back to it because you decided to get out and look for a job?"

"There ain't no jobs around here."

"You know this because you've looked around for one so extensively?"

"I've asked around." Her tone, like his, grew harsher with each exchange.

How long did he have to let her freeload before he could throw her out without guilt? He'd probably always have guilt where she was concerned. Intellectually, he knew he wasn't responsible for how she was. But some part of him would always think that her life probably would have been easier if he'd not been born to her when she was only a teenager with no real family of her own.

Easier in some ways, but possibly much harder in others. The thought surfaced with such a pang of remorse for past choices that he almost had to sit down.

Brent turned then and went back to the kitchen, stopping dead beside the fridge. His hands curled into fists at his sides. The temptation to reach for a beer to take the edge off this particular frustration grew stronger by the day.

The last thing he wanted was to spend the evening painting that room. His fists uncurled and he flexed his fingers. But it might be the only thing that kept him from satisfying this unbearable urge to drink. If he could just stay busy...

Just one. What can it hurt? Just one.

He envisioned himself opening the refrigerator door, not realizing that his hand reached for it in reality as well. He pictured himself grabbing one, pulling back the tab, and taking a long drink. He could feel the coolness of it on his throat, taste the blissful numbness it would foster. He could almost hear his mother's voice: *That's my boy! Now don't you feel better?*

He had reached for the handle but stopped short of pulling the door open.

No! He squeezed his eyes shut. This is not who he was anymore. Was it?

He reached into his back pocket for his wallet and fished out a little slip of paper. Thankfully, he'd had the forethought to find out if there was a local AA chapter here before he decided to come back. And if memory served, there was a meeting tonight. He unfolded the slip and read the information he had noted there. He checked his watch. It started five minutes ago.

Just in time.

ॐ

Brent slipped into a folding metal chair at the back of the room as the woman behind the lectern wrapped up her announcements and introduced a guest speaker. He relaxed against the back of the chair and released a burdened sigh.

A middle aged man next to him leaned closer. "Rough day?"

Brent nodded, feeling the burden lighten a little just from being here among others who understood his struggle on a personal level and shared the same goal to overcome it.

Had he ever struggled this hard against the impulse to return to his old ways of behaving?

It wasn't that he hadn't struggled before now. But God had blessed him tremendously by sending him into a church whose pastor, Pete Daly, shared a remarkably similar story. Brent had an extra strong safety net in those first years. Pete encouraged him to attend AA meetings and even became his sponsor. And he had struggled. But the struggle had been to break free of bad habits, old patterns of behavior, and destructive relationships.

The struggle felt so different now. Like he was struggling with who he was at his core. And with every day that passed, bringing him home at the end of increasingly long hours at the clinic to find Wanda in the same place, content to exist in the same circumstances she always had, he sank a little deeper into the mire he'd worked so hard to pull himself up out of. Every day he looked at her and saw where he came from and what she had raised him to become.

Therefore, if anyone is in Christ, he is a new creation; the old has gone, the new has come!

Brent closed his eyes and let the Word roll through his mind. He was a new creation. Until recently that was easy to believe.

He made so many plans on his way home. When he purchased the Denton place, it never occurred to him that it might ever become anything other than the haven he'd always wanted for a home. Certainly he hadn't thought that, within a month of moving in, it would become the place he wanted to avoid most. But as long as his mother sat parked on the hide-a-bed in his living room, smoking her cigarettes and drinking her beer, Brent would rather be anywhere but there.

Maybe he should have the satellite dish subscription cancelled. That would get her up.

The small group around him erupted in laughter and he tried to focus his attention on the speaker, a man in his sixties whom Brent vaguely recognized as a local resident. But his mind wandered to Audrey.

She loved him. That was something good that happened since he'd come back. She loved him, and the Lord seemed to be drawing her back to Him. It felt like a whole new chapter of his life was about to open up. Nothing stood between them now except the right timing, or lack thereof. That and his mother camped out on the couch bed in his living room.

The group around him broke into applause as the speaker finished his remarks and thanked them for letting him tell his story. Brent stood along with everyone else. The man who had spoken to him earlier clapped a friendly hand on his shoulder and gave a squeeze. Brent gave him a grateful smile and stepped into the aisle as he reached for his phone. He hadn't seen or heard from Audrey in a few days. He'd gone by her office today at lunch but it was empty. Maybe he'd call just to say hi. Thinking about the future with her brought him way more comfort than thinking about the past.

He scrolled through his contacts for her number, glancing up briefly to make sure the path was clear in front of him. A familiar form ahead registered the second he looked back at his phone, and he did a double take. Brent's thumb froze on the keypad, but he kept walking, leveling a challenging look at Bobby, who stood aside to let him pass without a word.

∂∞∕

Gertie had proven most reluctant to give up her shady spot on the hood of Audrey's car this afternoon when it came time to leave for the day. Not more than a few weeks ago she was ready to kill the animal and invite the whole town out for a barbeque. She suspected the usual cause of the goat's orneriness was just its personality, but it was obvious that the increasing heat and continuing drought was taking its toll even on Gertie.

After a few rounds of Audrey pushing, and Gertie defending her perceived right to the shady, breezy spot of her choice, she coaxed the goat down with a small tub of cool water. Her thirst quenched, she began nibbling at some dried leaves and managed to find a few weeds that were somehow surviving the weather.

Audrey arrived at the clinic to find Brent finishing up with his last patient of the day, a dog in need of a rabies vaccination. To her surprise Leanne was still there working behind the front desk, and George, a high-school volunteer, had just finished cleaning the last cage.

"It would appear there's nothing left for you to do," Brent said with a smile as he turned off the light in Lyndon's office.

"I bet the coffee pot needs rinsing," she said.

"You'd lose that bet."

"Really." Audrey flipped off the light switch in the hall. "I'm impressed."

"Well, what did you expect? Texas A&M University didn't give me a big fancy diploma for my good looks."

She grinned. "I wasn't about to suggest they did."

Brent continued down the hall to the next room, reached inside the open door, and switched off the light. Then he turned to face her.

He seemed so at home here, so natural. It was as if he'd been here the whole time. For a brief moment, just a split second, it felt as if the past ten years had never happened. Like she was eighteen again looking at the face of the boy she loved.

Audrey smiled and looked down. He'd done so much for them in the past several days. She couldn't help feeling now like the family tentacles were about to reach out and wind themselves around him, pulling him in to deal with their problems, even to hold them together somehow.

"Brent, could I ask you to do yet another favor for us?"

"Of course." He sounded surprised that she should ask. "What is it?

"I went home on my lunch hour today, and Mom told me to ask you to come over for dinner tonight."

"That's the favor?"

She looked at him.

"She thinks it might help if you come over and talk about the clinic with Dad. Maybe it will spark something in him and make him want to get back to work, or at least realize that he needs to."

"He's a lot worse, then?"

"It was one o'clock when I got there for lunch and he hadn't gotten out of bed yet. He's usually up by five-thirty every morning." She looked down again. "If he knows you're coming over, he'll get up and at least try. And maybe that's what he needs. Just to try a little."

"Maybe he needs to see someone. Like a doctor."

"Probably," Audrey agreed with a nod. "But how do you make someone go to the doctor?"

Audrey paused when Leanne, the vet tech, stuck her head around the corner and said she was headed home.

"Anyway," she continued quickly after the interruption, "if you could, we'd sure appreciate it. And even if it doesn't do any good at all, it's worth a try. Don't you think?"

Brent nodded. "I'll go on home and get cleaned up. Give me about an hour."

Audrey smiled. "Thanks. Oh, and bring your Mom, too, if she doesn't have any plans."

Brent laughed at that

"I don't know. She has a pretty hectic social schedule. But I'll ask."

❧

Her car was gone.

He noticed it first thing when he stepped out of his truck to check the mailbox. Wanda's beat up old car wasn't parked in its usual spot.

He tossed the stack of envelopes, each adorned with the big yellow forwarding address stickers, onto the seat beside him, thinking that maybe she'd gone out to look for a job. Maybe all she needed was a little time to regroup after a particularly hard time getting by. Maybe he'd been too hard on her last night when he came home to discover she hadn't done anything but sit in front of the television smoking and drinking all day.

Unless she returned home soon she wouldn't be going to dinner at Audrey's with him. He doubted she'd have gone, anyway.

Brent tossed the mail onto the kitchen counter as he went through to his bedroom. He stripped off dirty work clothes and added them to the already overflowing hamper. He showered quickly, dressed in a pair of jeans, a clean, blue chambray shirt, and a comfortable pair of boots.

On his way back through the kitchen he noticed a note and a key on the counter, right next to where the mail had landed.

He stopped, but hesitated to pick it up. He knew what it was. At least she had the courtesy to leave a note. A personal goodbye would have been nice, but at least she left something.

Brent sighed heavily, not understanding why the thought of his mother's departure disappointed him. He should be glad she was gone. Her leaving meant that there'd be no more covert smoking inside his house, no more cases of beer in the refrigerator tempting him at the end of a hard day. No doubt she'd taken any that were left with her.

He picked up the note and studied it. It said she hooked up with an old friend and they decided to pool their resources and see how they might be able to fare. She ended with a brief "thanks for everything," scribbled at the very bottom of the paper, as if it had been an afterthought.

Brent leaned back against the kitchen counter and closed his eyes, remembering suddenly the first time she'd run off.

He couldn't remember exactly how old he was, probably somewhere around six or seven. She'd been waiting tables at some old, dingy diner that didn't exist anymore, and her shift ended at ten. Even at that age he'd become accustomed to staying home alone after school. During the day the solitude never bothered him, but after the sun set he'd get a little scared. Sometimes he would fall asleep waiting, but he always heard her come in an hour or so after her shift was over.

One night he'd dozed off watching their tiny black and white T.V. and awoke much later to realize he hadn't heard her come in. He was careful to check her bed quietly, just in case she brought someone home. But she wasn't there. No one was. The numbers on the digital clock were still etched into his memory; three twenty-four a.m., and Brent had been alone in her filthy trailer.

Suddenly all he'd been able to hear were the shouts and cries of some act of domestic violence happening next door. Then some dogs started barking. The train whistled off in the distance.

Brent opened his eyes. Despite the fact that he was alone, standing in his own kitchen, he still fought the tears that threatened to spill over.

"Thanks for everything," he whispered bitterly.

Then it felt as if something reached down inside and took hold of his heart.

He had everything.

Sure he had a nice house and a nice truck. He had a good job, a steady paycheck. He was healthy. He even had Audrey, and she had a family who had practically taken him in and already relied on him as they might a son.

But he had still more than that. He had the Truth. He had Christ, and Christ had him.

There was a time in his life when he would have given anything to have a regular family, a mom, a dad, brothers and sisters, a home. Later there was a time when, just like his mother, the last thing he wanted was to be inconvenienced by someone needing him, by being held accountable for his life and his actions.

He'd thought himself free. Free from responsibility, free from rules that got in the way of doing exactly as he pleased.

But even then, even back when he lived his life according to the world's definition of freedom, thinking it exactly what he'd wanted, even then he'd hated his life. He'd hated himself. Deep down inside, and though she would never admit it, his mother must feel the same way.

Brent sat down at his small kitchen table, clutched

the handwritten note tightly in both hands, and began
to pray for her.

13

Audrey was right about Lyndon.

Brent was around him enough the past several weeks to know that Lyndon wasn't himself.

He had gotten out of bed for dinner; he'd even showered and dressed. He appeared to listen to everything Brent had to tell him about the clinic and even offered a few mechanical sounding suggestions. But it was evident that his behavior was for the sake of appearances. His heart and mind were somewhere else completely.

Brent stayed for two hours, trying his best to get Lyndon interested in the goings on at work. Paula had thanked him profusely for coming as he helped carry a few dishes from the dinner table to the kitchen. As much as he wanted to stay and do something that would make Lyndon snap out of this depression, it became increasingly obvious that Lyndon just wanted to go back to bed.

The sun hung low in the evening sky as Audrey walked him out to his truck, and an evening breeze had picked up that made being outside bearable, even pleasant, every now and then.

"Thanks for coming," Audrey said.

"Your mom already thanked me. Besides, I'm not sure how much good it did."

"I know it helped. Dad said he'd try to make it

into work tomorrow or the next day. That's something, isn't it?"

Brent nodded and studied her. She looked so at peace. Despite the unrest in the life of her family this past week, tranquility surrounded her. No, radiated from within. The breeze wisped her dark blonde hair back away from her beautiful face. She closed her eyes and breathed it in.

"Mmm. That feels good." She exhaled slowly and opened her eyes. "Makes me think that maybe one of these days fall really will get here."

He reached out and caught a strand of her hair, brushing it away from her face. "I guess it always does."

She smiled when his fingertips brushed against the soft skin of her cheek, then she leaned into his touch. She had completely forgotten the history between them, and how livid she had been at the sight of him just a couple of months ago. All had been forgiven. She trusted him entirely.

An image flashed in his mind, of Bobby's face when he'd seen him just last night at the local AA meeting. Then came another, of her face contorted with pain and then fear as Bobby turned on her in front of witnesses, and another of her arms raised to block the blows she assumed would follow. How many times had that happened to her in the privacy of her own home? The one place she should be safe and free from fear. How severely had she suffered at Bobby's hands?

Brent pulled her into an embrace and breathed deeply, but not contentedly as her arms slipped around his waist. The last thing he wanted to do was spoil this moment of peace and trust for her. But he had to tell her Bobby was out of jail. He didn't want her caught off guard should Bobby decide to come around when he wasn't here.

"It's too bad your mom couldn't make it." Her murmured words slipped out before he could speak.

"She took off today."

"What?" Audrey looked up at him

"She took off."

"To where?"

"I don't know." Brent leaned back against his truck loosening his hold, but not letting go. "She left a note on the kitchen counter. Said she met up with an old friend. She left the key, too, so I assume she's not intending to come back anytime soon."

"But why?" Audrey asked. "After all that work you did fixing up the house and a room for her. Why would she just leave, without even talking to you first?"

"That's what she does." He met and held her gaze for a moment. She was injured on his behalf. "Thanks for dinner. It was nice to have some place to go and someone to be with tonight."

"I'm sorry, Brent." The soft words soothed an ache inside him like he would have never believed before this moment. She laid her head on his shoulder. "You know you can come by here anytime. In fact, why don't you come over again tomorrow night? It'll get Dad out of bed again, for a few hours, anyway."

"That's real nice of you, Audrey, but you don't have to—"

"I mean it, Brent," she interrupted, raising her head to look at him again. "We're friends, right?"

He smiled. "Actually, I think we're a little more than that now."

"Then you should do this for me. We need you."

His smile widened and he hung his head and nodded as if in defeat. "You win," he said. "But one of these days you're gonna have to return the favor."

Her answering smile took his breath away.

If someone had told him eight or ten years ago that he would be so completely hooked by a woman he would have howled with laughter. He could imagine himself hooked on plenty of things, but never a woman. Not just one, anyway. But now...that life seemed hard to imagine now that he entertained the thought of spending the rest of his with her.

He kissed her gently, relishing the feel of her soft, warm mouth against his, inhaling the fragrance of her perfume, hearing the rhythm of her breath, committing every detail to memory. How she felt in his arms. The way he felt as she leaned into him, entrusting herself to him. Her tender response stirred something he had never experienced before. Plenty of times he'd felt physical desire for a woman, but never this desire to care for, protect and defend.

As Audrey pulled her mouth from his, nuzzled her face into the curve of his neck and breathed a contented sigh, the image of Bobby flashed again.

"Audrey..."

"Oh! I didn't tell you." She looked up at him, grinning even wider than before. "Carlene and Jim got married yesterday."

He blinked, not sure he'd heard right. "What?"

She nodded. "I went with them to the courthouse at lunch to be a witness."

"I wasn't aware they were even dating."

Brent tried to imagine Carlene married, and to Jim Carlton. He didn't know Jim very well, but he didn't figure Carlene for the sort of woman who would appeal to him. Jim seemed steady and predictable, whereas Carlene was impulsive and sometimes rash. Jim struck Brent as a man of few words, and Carlene had a tendency to talk incessantly. There had been a lot about Carlene that had appealed to him back in school, her impulsiveness had kept him entertained. She was fun, always up for a challenge, and definitely a no-strings-attached kind of girl. And now she was married.

A grin spread slowly at the thought.

"She's expecting." Audrey's statement sounded muffled against his collar as she nestled into the curve of his neck again.

"A baby?"

She lifted her head and looked at him, one eyebrow arched upward in mock concern, as if to ask, *what else?*

He gave a low chuckle. "I almost can't imagine Carlene Fletcher as a wife and mother."

"I think we'll need to call her Carlene Carlton from now on."

He couldn't suppress a laugh at the sound of that. "Carlene Carlton." He repeated the name. "Well. She's always been full of surprises."

"You started to tell me something?"

He felt his grin fade as he expelled a heavy sigh. Her expression fell to mirror his.

"I saw Bobby last night."

"What?" She straightened in his arms. "Where?"

Brent looked down. He knew he couldn't say where. Though he didn't think Bobby deserved any consideration whatsoever, he couldn't divulge the fact that he'd seen him at an AA meeting. That was Bobby's business to tell.

"Did you say anything to him?"

He shook his head, thankful she didn't press further. "No, but he's out of jail. And I wanted you to be aware. Just in case..."

Just in case...just in case, what?

He didn't even want to entertain an idea of what could happen if Bobby came around drunk and mad. Audrey once told him that the reason she never pressed charges before was because she was afraid to make him even more angry than he would ordinarily be. And now she'd done it. She'd had him arrested and charged. No one thought he'd be back out and among them so soon. And now he could imagine the very real danger she was in.

She knew it too. Tears welled in her eyes, and the tranquil peace that had emanated from her only seconds ago dissipated like a phantom.

"What should I do?" she whispered.

He shook his head and pulled her close. He had no idea.

"Trust God."

∂∽

Audrey had just placed a fresh glass of iced tea on the end table next to her dad when she heard the car door slam outside.

Her father's progress had slipped a little since he got home from work last night and now he stared blankly at the old western playing on the television. The noises from her mother's preparation of supper in the kitchen continued despite the growing sense of dread welling up inside Audrey.

Brent had called just a few moments ago to report

to Lyndon, who had taken the day off, the status of the clinic, and to say that he'd be heading home to tend to a few things there before coming over for dinner.

Carlene almost always called before she came over.

Audrey knew only one person who would be dropping by her house tonight, and he could only have one reason for coming.

She glanced quickly back at her father. He hadn't even noticed her presence in the room, so she opened the front door and stepped out onto the porch. Her intuition had been right. It was Bobby's pickup parked on the front curb.

She took a deep breath.

Her father sat mostly unresponsive inside the house, and she had no idea what sort of reaction he might have to a confrontation with Bobby, but it couldn't be good. Brent was nowhere near. This situation she would have to handle herself.

"Lord, give me strength," she whispered quietly.

Countless times, she'd uttered that phrase in exasperation at some situation, usually regarding Bobby. Before now it had just been an expression, something to say. Now, she realized it was a prayer. She meant it. She earnestly needed God to provide her with some extra courage. Any courage at all would be good.

Bobby came slowly up the front walk and stopped at the foot of the porch steps. He had another bouquet in his hands. This was a nice one, though, wrapped in tissue paper and ribbons like it had come from a florist and not grabbed as an afterthought at some convenience store at the same time he bought his case of beer. He was dressed in his nicest jeans, starched stiff, freshly polished boots, and a colorful button down shirt. She could smell his cologne from where he stood.

She folded her arms across her chest to try and stop the trembling of her hands.

"These are for you," Bobby said, holding the flowers out to her.

"I don't want them."

He withdrew the bouquet and looked down, picking at the greenery nervously.

"I don't know where to start," he said. "I don't know what to say."

"You know what to say, Bobby," Audrey snapped. "Just say what you always say. Tell me how sorry you are, that you don't know what came over you, that you'll never lay a hand on me again. Oh, maybe you could tell me that you'll quit drinking if I want you to. Or that you've changed."

Bobby looked up at her, tears filling his eyes and threatening to spill silently over.

"I'm sorry, Audrey," he said. "I don't know how to make you believe me."

One tear did fall then. It rolled down his cheek and dripped off his chin, landing on the flowers he still clutched.

"I came back here intending to be a better man, baby. I was gonna be what you needed me to be. The kind of man you'd marry and trust to be good to you, to take care of you. I don't know what gets into me. I don't know where the anger comes from. It just comes, and then I take it out on you. I don't mean to, I just..."

He looked up at her as if for some reassurance, but Audrey remained unmoved. A peaceful strength seemed to permeate her at that moment. Her hands stopped trembling and her heart stopped racing.

Her first thought was that with such a sudden and bold new confidence she ought to snatch the bouquet from his hands and clip him over the head with it. Her next thought was that her earlier prayer had been answered just in time, because not long ago his next tactic would have worked.

"I love you, baby." That much was true. In his own crazy way, he did love her. "You know I do, or I wouldn't be here now beggin' you to forgive me."

"Bobby, just—"

"Just hear me out." Bobby held up one hand as he interrupted her. "Just give me a chance to show you that I can change. I know I can, I just don't think I can do it alone. I just need to try a little harder and maybe get a little help. Please, baby. Please let me come home."

"I gave you your chance."

"What?"

"I said I gave you your chance. When you came back I didn't call the police. I let you cut my yard and paint my living room. I let you back into my life, Bobby. I gave you a chance to prove yourself. All I got was attacked in front of my family and friends."

Bobby glanced down, all remorse and clearly at a loss for words. As always, he thought quickly and came up with another tactical maneuver.

"We had some good times together, didn't we?" he asked looking back up at her.

Audrey didn't respond.

"Didn't we?"

Unable to deny that there had been times when she'd been happy with him, she nodded.

"You loved me, baby, I know you did. Just think

back on those times," he said. "Those times are worth something, aren't they?"

"Like what, Bobby? Like a beating every now and then?"

"No! That's not what I mean, baby. I just don't know how to get myself right. I don't want to be this way, I don't. I know exactly what it's like for you when I go crazy like that. The last thing I ever wanted was to be like my old man, and I turned out just like him, and I hate myself for it. You're the best thing that's ever happened to me, and I hate myself for all the things I've done. I *hate* myself for…"

He couldn't even say what he'd done. But she knew that's what he hated himself for most.

"You need to leave now, Bobby." Her voice was soft, but there was no uncertainty in it.

"Audrey, please..."

He was crying now. Really crying. She'd never seen him quite so desperate with self loathing. And she knew what he was saying was true.

"Bobby, go now," she said more sternly. "I mean it. You've used your last chance. Don't come back. Next time I'll be the one who calls the police."

Bobby stared silently as if in disbelief, or maybe shock, for a moment. As the finality of her words sank in, grief registered on his face, then acceptance. He nodded almost imperceptibly and seemingly to himself. It was over, and he agreed.

"And so you should." He handed the bouquet up to her and when she wouldn't accept it, he laid it on the steps at her feet, then he turned to walk away.

"I'm with Brent now."

Bobby stopped and tensed, but didn't turn around.

"So don't think you can come back around and try

to change my mind again. Don't come back."

She heard him expel a long breath. Then he continued to his truck, got in and drove away.

After he'd gone, Audrey stood staring at the flowers. She should probably at least pick them up and throw them away. But something inside her feared to even touch them, as if doing so might somehow reconnect the tie she'd just severed.

She stood for another moment debating the legitimacy of such a superstitious idea, then the excitement of the stand she'd just taken got the better of her and she smiled.

She retrieved the flowers and turned back toward the front door. Now she was free. And she wanted to tell Brent all about it.

14

"So. Married life seems to agree with you." Audrey wadded up her paper towel and tossed it into the garbage can by the door, then turned to lean back against the counter as Carlene finished touching up her lip gloss. Carlene actually blushed at that and Audrey laughed. "It does, doesn't it?"

Carlene pressed her lips together, twisted the cap back onto her tube of gloss and dropped it into her cosmetic case. "I'm not saying that there hasn't been some adjustment. But, yes. Jim treats me well. He told me he wants me to stay home after the baby comes."

Audrey arched her brows, trying to imagine Cosmo-girl Carlene's reaction when Jim made that statement. "And you said...?"

She shrugged and looked down. "I always thought I'd have to work when I had kids. Never even considered the possibility that I might not have to. But we've been looking at nursery furniture and baby clothes, and...I don't know. I want to stay home."

"So, I'll have to get used to someone else coming in and speculating about the weather every day." As if to illustrate her point a huge clap of thunder sounded outside. Audrey felt tears sting. She was happy for Carlene. But now it seemed like everything was changing so fast. Her peaceful little life of the past year had been turned over and shaken around, and there was no way to predict where the pieces would fall.

Carlene grinned. "Not for long."

She furrowed her brow. "What?"

"Well," Carlene drawled, completely herself again, "I think we can all see where things are going with you and Brent. You'll be married soon enough."

Brent had been a constant companion to her and her folks for the past two weeks. Her dad's depression had improved some with a visit to the doctor and several counseling sessions with the family's pastor. It was Friday and her father had been to work every day this week.

Brent thought her parents could manage a meal without them tonight while they met up with Jim and Carlene for dinner at the Prickly Pear.

Audrey sighed and smiled.

"See!" Carlene poked her in the ribs, then pulled the restroom door open. "I knew it! Hey, is that Barbie Bledsoe?"

Audrey looked up as the restroom door closed.

It was. Her heart plummeted.

Brent and Barbie had been rather long term in high school. Long term for him, anyway. They had dated off and on for a whole school year, not that Brent hadn't gone and done whatever he pleased when she wasn't around. But Barbie had never complained.

And there she stood, as tall and tanned and blonde and beautiful as ever, looking at Brent as if she couldn't get enough of him. Then she hugged him.

"Well, come on." Carlene grabbed her by the arm. "Get over there and stake your claim, girl."

Audrey lurched forward, propelled by Carlene's grip on her elbow, and was deposited at Brent's side just as Barbie pulled herself halfway out of the embrace to gaze on Brent some more.

"I've been fine, Brent." Barbie laughed. "Just fine. And how long have you been back in town?"

"Since June." Brent looked sincerely pleased to see Barbie. His face softened in a way that made Audrey want to remind him somehow that she was here. But then Brent let go of Barbie. He slid an arm around Audrey and pressed his hand to the small of her back. "I'm working for Audrey's dad now."

"You're a veterinarian?"

Brent nodded.

"And I knew the two of you would eventually end up together." Barbie hugged Audrey. "I think we all sort of knew it, didn't we, Carlene?"

"I always thought she could do better." Carlene's comment was tempered with a grin.

Barbie's gaze would occasionally flicker to Audrey or Carlene. She glanced briefly at Jim when Brent introduced him as Carlene's husband. But her primary focus remained on Brent. And who could blame her? Brent was so much more. The change in him was so complete that one could tell he was a different man, a better man, just by looking.

Relief nearly overwhelmed Audrey when Barbie was joined by a thirty-something year old man hauling an infant carrier in one hand, and a short chain of twin boys by the other. She introduced him as her husband, then she introduced her three children. She and her husband had a brief conference before he handed her the check and the infant carrier. He took the car keys and the twins, one by each hand, and headed for the parking lot.

Barbie turned back to Brent as the baby started to cry.

Brent stepped closer to the carrier and peeked under the lightweight, pink cotton receiving blanket. "How old is she?"

"Eight weeks," Barbie said, gently lifting the baby up out of the carrier to cradle her. She began to sway back and forth, talking softly to the infant, who immediately began to quiet.

"She's so tiny," Brent said reaching out to stroke the baby's small hand with his finger. He laughed, clearly amazed, when the little one's fingers closed tightly around his.

Audrey smiled as she watched Brent become completely entranced by the little baby girl. She meant to look back at the baby, but she ended up doing a double take back at Brent. Tears filled his eyes.

"Could I get you to hold her for just a minute while I go and pay our bill?" Barbie had asked a question, but clearly did not mean to wait for a reply, having already settled the baby in his arms and turned to the table beside them to shuffle through her diaper bag in search of her wallet.

"It'll just take a minute. I'll be right back." Barbie headed to the cash register leaving everything but the check and her wallet in Brent's safekeeping.

Brent didn't even seem to notice she had gone. The little person in his arms captivated him. He couldn't take his eyes off her as he gently stroked her face and hands. When the baby turned her head toward him and started to root around in the front of his shirt, he laughed softly. But tears were there just beneath the surface, and when his smile faded his expression became unreadable.

"Thanks so much." Barbie took the baby, murmuring a few soft words to her as she nestled her into her carrier. Then, with the speed and efficiency of a woman with three small children, she buckled the little safety belt, slung the diaper bag over one shoulder and hoisted the carrier up onto one hip.

"We're just here visiting my folks for the weekend." Barbie smiled. "But it's been a long day and the boys are getting cranky. We should get together sometime."

Brent nodded as she turned to go, then he stepped silently to the cash register and paid their bill.

The gentle roll of thunder blended together with the soft sounding wash of rain on the roof, and a collective sigh sounded around the dining room. Rain. Several people stood to glance out the windows. Everyone smiled, except Brent who didn't seem to notice until they stepped outside under the front awning.

The air already smelled cleaner and Audrey took a deep breath, then let it out slowly. Brent stuck his hand out from underneath the protective cover, letting the rain wash over it. Completely lost in his thoughts.

She laid a gentle hand on his arm. "Brent...?"

Out of nowhere came Carlene, one shoe in each hand, running past them straight out into the shower. She threw her arms open wide and spun around.

"It's raining!" she shouted as the rain soaked her hair and her dress. It made a very unsophisticated sight, but so characteristic of who Carlene really was inside.

Jim came to stand beside them, watching Carlene with a captivated smile. He glanced at Brent, who chuckled at some secret "guy" code that seemed to pass between them.

"See y'all later." Then Jim jogged out into the rain,

getting to their car just in time to open the door for Carlene.

A smile still lingered from watching Carlene's antics. She turned to Brent to find him studying her. He reached for her hand and together they made a dash through the shower for his truck. He opened the door for her and she climbed in, breathless and laughing, pushing her fingers through her now damp hair. A few seconds later he climbed in behind the steering wheel and ruffled his short wet hair, sending droplets everywhere.

In a second he turned inward again, pushing his key into the ignition and starting the engine, steering out of the parking lot and onto the highway back toward her house. He took a deep breath as if to say something, but then let it out silently. A few times he seemed on the verge of beginning, but the silence lingered as he turned off the highway and into the residential part of town. Block after block and house after house passed by outside as his discomfort seemed to increase.

"What is it, Brent?" she asked gently, apprehensively, trying to eradicate the image of Barbie Bledsoe's infatuated expression a few minutes ago, as well as the tender look Brent had returned.

He turned his head slightly in her direction, but kept his eyes on the road. Then he exhaled as if he'd been holding his breath for years. "You know firsthand what kind of guy I was back then." His voice sounded tight and pained, almost defensive. "I didn't care about anything or anyone. I didn't have a clue."

He paused and took another deep breath, pulling his truck up against the curb in front of her house and shifting it into park. "I slept with a lot of girls."

Some old part of her bristled at his words even though she had always known the truth in them. She didn't really want to revisit that part of his past. She preferred to think of him as he was now. Totally hers. But withdrawing from him would probably be the worst thing she could do at this moment, so she unbuckled her seat belt and slid across the seat, closer to him, keeping silent while he struggled.

"I was lucky for a long time," he continued. "No 'accidents,' no diseases. But then I got a girl pregnant."

Audrey froze. This was a possibility she had never considered.

"You have a child?" Her tone sounded disappointed, even to her. She looked down at her knees before glancing back at him.

He didn't look at her. He just shook his head as tears filled his eyes. "I had a child."

His hand rested on the seat between them and she covered it with hers as realization dawned on her. "You lost a child?" She could barely push the words past the ache in her throat as memories of her lost child began to swirl.

Brent took hold of her hand, intertwined his fingers with hers and held on to it tightly, bringing it to his lips and pressing a kiss to the back. He shook his head again and took a deep breath, finally looking at her with tearful eyes.

"I didn't know what to do." He glanced away again. "I was young and stupid. I was drunk most all the time. I could barely hold a job. I certainly didn't want to be bothered by any kind of commitment, and there I was faced with fatherhood."

He paused and looked down. A tear fell and landed on her hand. He wiped it away with his thumb.

"When she told me, I got mad. As far as I was concerned, it was her problem. It didn't need to involve me. But she told me, and then I was involved. And I got mad."

He squeezed his eyes shut and gave his head a shake. "She was crying when she left. And I was stunned. But after the initial shock wore off, I thought maybe it could be my chance. To change. To break the insane cycle of my life...my mother's life. To at least be there, so the kid wouldn't have to grow up wondering who I was and what I looked like."

He pressed his lips together and stared out the windshield for a long, silent moment before she laid a hand on his arm to bring him back.

"Anyway." With a small shake of his head he continued. "For three days she wouldn't return my calls. When I finally found her at her dorm..." He swallowed hard. "She told me she'd had an abortion, and she never wanted to see me again. And she never did. Not around town, not at parties. I heard she dropped out of school and went back home.

"And I started drinking harder than ever. I managed to convince myself the kid was better off...just like I'd always thought I would have been better off–my mother would have been better off...you...and so many others...the world would have been better off–if I'd never been born."

Audrey couldn't stop an involuntary gasp. So much heartache hounded her, used by one man, then abused by another. But with his last words her heart absolutely broke. She'd never known–never even imagined–that Brent had felt that way. All these years she'd remembered him as arrogant and insensitive, not caring how his behavior affected anyone else.

"Oh, Brent," she breathed his name.

"I always imagined the baby was a girl," he whispered.

Silence descended on them before he finally took a deep shuddering breath. "My own child. And if I just hadn't spoken so harshly to a girl I'd already treated so wrongly. Now there's not anything I'd rather have than a family. But sometimes I think that I had my chance, you know? I had a kid, and I..." He ended with a shrug and a slight shake of his head. "Maybe having a family is too much for me to ask now."

The view out the windshield was blurred as much by her tears as by the rain that continued to fall in large soft drops. Another distant rumble of thunder sounded as the world around them was finally washed clean. She sniffed.

"I'm sorry, Audrey." Brent's low, deep voice went right to her heart. "It's been on my mind a lot lately. I just had to tell somebody. I thought you should know...what all I've done."

"Oh, Brent." She leaned closer still and placed her palms on either side of his face. He was still convicting himself for so many things he did before he came to know the Lord. How could he not? He had freely admitted to her that he knew better than to live his life the way he had, even before he became a Christian. But he, better than anyone, should know that only God could have ever broken those chains anyway.

She pushed a short lock of his hair off his forehead. "You're not that person anymore. Remember?"

He looked at her as if searching for forgiveness in her eyes, and finally smiled through his pain and nodded.

"You're a Christian now. That all by itself makes you a different person." She slid hands down to his shoulders, then down his arms to his hands which she clasped in her own. "I can see the changes in you, Brent. Everyone can see the changes in you. Barbie could see the changes in you, and she has no idea what's happened in your life these past years."

He raised his gaze from their joined hands to her eyes.

"Did you think it would change the way I feel about you?" The breath nearly caught in her throat at the desperate look in his eyes. That's exactly what he had thought. "Because it doesn't."

He let go of her hands and reached for her, pulling her the rest of the distance across the seat until he embraced her. So close she could feel his heart beating.

"Do you still love me, Audrey? After all this time. Really?" Brent asked, a finger under her chin gently tilting her head back up to look at him. "Because I love you."

Audrey bit her tongue to keep the tears from coming, but it was a futile attempt. Her vision blurred as she listened to his sweet words.

"I want you to marry me, Audrey, and come to live with me." Brent choked up a little before he continued. "I want us to have children and, someday, grandchildren. I want us to be a family, even though I know it's probably the last thing I deserve."

A sob erupted from her, catching her completely off guard.

Of course he wanted a family—children. She buried her face in her hands and sobbed again, squeezing her eyes shut against an image of Bobby's enraged expression above her, remembering how she had curled up into a ball trying desperately to protect the child inside from his furious kicks. The tearing pain a few hours later assured her that she had failed.

The warmth of Brent's arms closed around her. "Audrey?"

"I don't know if I can," she whispered.

His arms slackened about her. "What?" He sounded as if someone had just knocked the air out of him.

"Have children." She clarified, sniffing and wiping her tears away. "I don't know if I can have children. I had a miscarriage last year..."

"Oh, Audrey." The compassion in his tone prompted another tear to fall as he cradled her face in his hands. Then he kissed her.

His mouth was soft and familiar, but this experience with him was still all new and almost too good to be true. He was completely here with her, wanting her alone, and no other woman would do. He loved her. He wanted to marry her. Finally.

"Will you marry me, Audrey?" He murmured against her skin, pressing small kisses softly to her cheek, then brushing her hair off her shoulder to press a series of warm kisses to her neck, just below her earlobe. "Will you come live in that big old house with me?" His mouth covered hers again once, then twice. "Please?"

She nodded as more tears flowed. "Yes."

He let out a long, relieved sounding breath as she pressed her forehead to his. "I don't have a ring." He mumbled the admission. "I'm maybe not as prepared as I should have been."

"Oh." She sniffed and raised her hands to wipe away her tears. "Well then, forget it."

He straightened and stared at her, a slow smile emerging to mirror hers. Then he kissed her again as the rain continued to fall softly outside.

ৎৡ৹৶

"So when can we tell them?" Brent murmured in Audrey's ear as they followed her parents down the church aisle to their regular pew in the center of the sanctuary.

She hadn't been to church for a regular Sunday morning worship service in a few years, and she was just a bit nervous about being seen here by everyone after so long an absence. Especially considering that her moral conduct during that absence had been significantly less than stellar.

"I don't know," she replied quietly, a smile touching her mouth. "When do I get a ring?"

Brent paused and looked at her as she took her seat beside her mother. He grinned.

"How 'bout we drive to Austin this afternoon and shop for one?"

"Shop for what?" Paula leaned over and asked.

"An engagement ring," Brent said.

Paula looked from Brent to Audrey, who couldn't contain a giddy smile.

"Must have been some night at the Prickly Pear," she said just before she leaned the other direction and began to whisper in her husband's ear.

Her father turned his head to look over at her. But he wore a satisfied smile, the first one she'd seen on him since the fire, and almost as if this had been the plan the whole time. They approved this time.

Brent's arm slipped around her shoulders and she

nestled there basking in his affection. As the organ prelude swelled, the small choir filled the loft, and the preacher took his place on the platform, her heart soared. It felt good to be back, natural, and as she sang, and prayed, and listened to the sermon, she began to feel as if she'd never been gone at all. By the end of the service peaceful joy enveloped her. The Lord had taken her back. Everything would be all right.

As they stood to leave, Brent took her hand.

"You never did tell me if you thought going to Austin today would be a good idea."

"You mean to shop for a ring?"

He nodded.

"Oh, I guess it would be all right." She teased him with an exaggeratedly put upon sigh. "Just remember..." Audrey stopped short at the last thing she expected to see today, or any day, for that matter.

Sudden tension emanated from Brent and his hand tightened around hers. She glanced up to find him staring at the same person who had halted her in her tracks.

Bobby Kerr leaned against the wall at the very back of the sanctuary.

His eyes met Audrey's, then he looked at Brent. His dark gaze dropped to their linked hands, then down to the floor where it remained as they passed him on their way out. Audrey's spine was rigid with the tension she felt, and she had to fight hard against the impulse to look back over her shoulder.

"You OK?" Brent asked once they'd reached his pickup.

"I knew he'd be back," she said through gritted teeth. "I knew it. I knew he'd never just leave and let me move on and live my life in peace."

Brent pulled her close and held her.

"Don't worry," he said. "We'll handle this. We'll do whatever we have to do. We'll go the police, and get a restraining order."

Audrey nodded, content to be in his arms and so glad to have him on her side.

"We can handle this," he said quietly.

⮞⭗⭘

Brent checked his watch as he slid into what was becoming their regular booth at the Prickly Pear. He was fifteen minutes early. He ordered iced tea to drink while he waited. After the waitress left his table he realized he was grinning.

He'd been doing that a lot the past few weeks. It surprised him, too, because he'd never behaved this way over a woman. But he couldn't seem to stop it. He was getting married. To Audrey who was not only the woman he loved, but also his best friend.

When everyone else dismissed him as trash on account of his mother's lifestyle, Audrey had been a steadfast friend. She had never seen anything but him—not his mother and her string of live-in boyfriends, not the run-down, filthy trailer he'd lived in. She'd only seen him, independent of all that, and she loved him. Only God knew why.

Even when he returned after a ten-year absence, she couldn't hide how she still felt about him. She tried hard to be stoic, but Audrey was an emotional woman. Every little thing she felt showed clearly on her face…in her eyes.

He loved that about her.

He glanced down at his watch. Almost no time

had elapsed.

"Waiting for someone?"

Brent's grin faded and every muscle tensed. He recognized the voice. And the question sounded like a challenge despite the cordial tone. His pulse quickened and he forced himself to take slow, deep deliberate breaths.

"As a matter of fact, I am." He didn't want to fight, so he forced an easy tone. But when he looked up, Bobby refused to look away.

Bobby shifted his weight and looked down. Clearly he had not come here to cause trouble either, and as far as Brent could tell, he was completely sober.

"Mind if I sit for a minute?"

Brent clenched his teeth. He minded. He'd like nothing better than to run Bobby out of town permanently, but not before punching him a few times for good measure.

"Just for a minute," Bobby said.

Brent nodded and took a deep breath, his pulse slowing at the realization that Bobby hadn't come here to confront him. "What's this about? Audrey is supposed to meet me in a few minutes, and I'd rather you were gone when she gets here."

Bobby slid into the opposite side of Brent's booth and waved the waitress away when she came to ask if she could get him anything to drink.

"I've been trying to keep my distance from Audrey." Bobby looked down and began picking at a callus on the palm of his hand. He kept his voice low.

"You mean you've been trying to keep your distance by showing up at her house and stalking her at church?"

Bobby glanced up at Brent briefly, then he

redirected his attention to the callus again.

"I heard y'all got engaged."

"That's right."

Bobby nodded. "I know I'm not what Audrey needs. I'm the last thing anyone needs. And I know she doesn't believe me when I tell her I want to change. Why should she? I never change." He paused and took a breath. "I never intended to be the kind of man I am."

"Listen, Bobby." The disdain in Brent's heart was clear by the tone of his voice. "Audrey and me, we're gonna get married. She's got a ring on her finger, and we're making wedding plans. Don't think you're going to come back around and change her mind, because I won't let that happen."

Bobby shook his head and leaned on the table.

"That's not what I'm doing," he said earnestly. "I swear it. This isn't about Audrey. Not directly. That's why I wanted to talk to you when she wasn't around."

"If it's not about Audrey, why are you talking to me about it at all?"

"Because you've done it," Bobby said quickly. "You and me, we're a lot alike. At least we used to be. But you've...you're somebody now. You're different. You're a better man, a respectable man, and I want to know how you did it. I've tried so hard and nothing about me ever changes. But you did...

"The reason I've been at the church is because I heard you go there now. I heard you believe in God now. I thought maybe that's what made the difference. I'm not stalking Audrey."

Brent sat up straight and leaned back against the seat. The shock probably registered plainly on his face, but he couldn't cover it. Bobby wanted to know about God? About Christ and salvation?

Audrey's past declarations of his deceitful ways streamed steadily through his mind, at odds with the resonation in his soul. The skin on the back of his neck prickled. But Brent narrowed his eyes. If she were here, she'd see right through him. She'd see this encounter for what it probably really was: Bobby trying, by any means necessary, to work his way back into her life.

Considering honestly changing his ways and coming to Christ was one of the most uncharacteristic things Bobby could do. Even if he tried, Brent couldn't imagine a more unlikely source for questions that might lead to salvation.

Except maybe himself about six years ago.

The breath left his chest, as if someone had stuck a hand inside, wrapped thick fingers around his heart and began to squeeze. He'd been right there in Bobby's place once. Who was he to doubt God's direction in the life of another?

Lord? Is it you?

Brent swallowed and started to speak but found his voice was thick and hoarse. He cleared his throat. "When was the last time you drank?"

The look of relief on Bobby's face erased all doubt about his motivation. His eyes filled with tears, then he smiled a little. "Not since the day I was arrested."

Brent looked down. Then he looked around the diner. There had to be someone here more qualified to lead this discussion than he was. He still struggled so hard.

"The other night at the AA meeting, they gave me this." Bobby reached into his shirt pocket, pulled out a small gold medallion and held it up. The phrase *one day at a time* stamped clearly on it.

Brent reached for his keys and showed Bobby the

fob he carried in which his own chip was displayed. "Six years for me. No, six and a half." The amendment gave him a measure of comfort. He had struggled hard lately, but he hadn't failed. And in six more months' time, he'd be able to pick up another medallion. One with seven years stamped into it.

"They suggested I find a sponsor..." Bobby let his voice trail off as he dropped his chip back into his pocket, then he hazarded a glance back up at Brent.

Brent understood what he was asking and shook his head. "I'm not sure that would be such a good idea."

Bobby nodded and swallowed hard. "I know there's no reason for anyone to want to help me, especially you. But I just...I can't..." He shook his head as his voice trailed off.

He couldn't put it into words, but Brent knew what he was trying to say. Bobby was desperate to change. There was no way he'd be asking him for help otherwise.

Brent ran a finger over his six year medallion. Pete Daly had been his sponsor, and he never would have made it this far if he hadn't had Pete to confide in. Brent didn't want to hear Bobby's story over and over. Especially as it related to Audrey. But if Bobby was really going to do this, he needed someone. Someone who had been there.

"I need to talk to Audrey about it."

Bobby paused and looked back down, the muscles in his jaw began to twitch. "I never wanted to hurt Audrey." His voice was low and thick. "Never. I love Audrey. And even she'll tell you that when I wasn't drinking we had a good life together. As long as I'm sober, I'm fine."

Bobby wasn't fine, drunk or sober. But how was Brent supposed to tell him that? What words would he use to convince Bobby that what he needed was not merely to stay sober? What could he say to persuade him that he wouldn't be able to stay sober relying on his own strength anyway?

Brent had never had the opportunity or inclination to witness so boldly to anyone before. Fear seized him. What if this wasn't really what Bobby came for? Maybe his gut feeling was wrong. Maybe to mention Christ and salvation now would serve only to drive Bobby away, thinking Brent was some kind of over-zealous religious freak.

"What changed you?" Bobby's question was like a word straight from God.

Brent's pounding heart began to calm and his mind to clear.

"God."

Brent paused and waited for a disdainful laugh or a snide mocking reply, but none came. Bobby's gaze remained unwavering on Brent's face. Clearly this was exactly what he'd come for. "Do you believe in God?"

"Yeah," Bobby answered. "I guess I've always believed in God."

"I always believed in God, too," Brent said.

Then he took a deep breath and plunged in.

He told Bobby of his youthful perception of God as a distant dictator whose function was to make rules that no normal person could possibly live by. He told of his exploits in College Station and how he'd come to be living as all but a vagrant. Then he told Bobby about the experience he'd had in the parking lot of the bar the night he became aware that God's grace at some point extended even to a faithless loser like him.

During Brent's narration, Bobby had leaned closer, his hands balled into fists on the table in front of him. After Brent finished, Bobby sat still, breathing deeply, tension radiating off him like the little heat waves rising off the blacktop parking lot outside.

"Do you think that same thing could happen to me?" Bobby finally asked.

"I think it is happening to you," Brent said.

Bobby swallowed hard, looked down and shifted in his seat. "I want to think about it."

Brent glanced down at his watch. Audrey was ten minutes late. He looked up to find Bobby watching him.

"I'll go," Bobby said. "I guess she'll be here any minute now. Is there any way I could talk to you about this more sometime?"

Brent nodded as Bobby slid out of the booth. He stood for a moment, awkwardly. Then he extended his hand toward Brent.

Brent hesitated. Shaking Bobby's hand now would change everything between them. It might change everything between him and Audrey, too. And how could he? After all the pain and suffering Bobby had inflicted on her.

Therefore, if anyone is in Christ, he is a new creation; the old has gone, the new has come!

The scripture that had tethered him to Christ rolled through his heart. If it had been true for him, then it could hold true for Bobby as well. Otherwise it wasn't the Truth at all.

He's almost there. The still small voice whispered. *Help him along. If you don't, no one will.*

Brent nodded, reached out and shook Bobby's hand.

"Thanks." Bobby turned to go, but stopped short.

Audrey stood just inside the door, the look on her face already calling Brent a traitor.

15

"Don't get irrational," Audrey whispered to herself. "Don't jump to conclusions."

But how many different conclusions could there possibly be to explain the sight of Brent shaking hands with the man he nearly beat senseless a few weeks ago on her behalf? The man who had threatened an attack on her in public, and who had attacked her repeatedly over the last several years in private.

Should she stalk over to the table where Brent sat, confront them both and demand an explanation of their apparent new friendship? Should she turn and leave? Should she just stand here and wait for something to happen? And what on earth could the two of them have been discussing so cordially?

The questions faded, silenced by the increasing intensity of her heart rate as Bobby began walking slowly toward her. She sucked in her breath and held it as he approached. She wanted to squeeze her eyes shut until she felt him pass, but she couldn't seem to move. Closer he came, until he was within five steps of being able to touch her. Four steps. Three steps more and he would be able to grab her by the arm and drag her out with him. She wanted to stand her ground. To call upon that uncharacteristic courage she'd found a few nights ago as she'd faced him on her front porch. But the sight of Brent shaking Bobby's hand struck a blow nearly as powerful as any Bobby had ever dealt her. She took a step back as Bobby closed the distance.

"Audrey," he said in greeting, nodding slightly as he passed her.

The scent of his cologne lingered after he'd gone. Audrey could smell it when she started to breathe again. Memories of him washed over her. She closed her eyes, and then opened them a few seconds later, focusing her attention on Brent who looked at her pleadingly.

The clatter of pans dropped in the kitchen brought her back to full awareness of where she stood. But the dining room was silent. One glance around confirmed her fear that they had become a spectacle. Every pair of eyes was trained on her, waiting to see her reaction.

She swallowed hard, took a deep breath, turned and walked out.

Brent would follow her, just like that first day when he'd followed her across the parking lot to her car. This time she waited for him.

She stood under the front awning watching Bobby's truck turn out of the parking lot and onto Main Street. She squinted against the glare reflected off of windshields by the early evening sun, then she glanced down at the engagement ring on her hand.

"Let me explain." The gentleness of Brent's voice soothed her mounting anger, but tears still stung. She blinked and bit her tongue in an effort to hold them back, silently cursing her emotions.

"He came to me," Brent started. "I was waiting for you, and he came over and asked if he could talk to me. He wanted to be gone by the time you got here."

Audrey began twisting the engagement ring around on her finger, but she remained silent.

Somehow it didn't comfort her to know that, whatever the topic of conversation, it was intended to be a secret kept from her. Despite her best efforts, a tear fell and rolled down her cheek.

"Oh, Audrey." His voice was as gentle as she'd ever heard it. "What are you thinking? Do you think I'm gonna become best buddies with him now? Don't you know I can still barely stand the sight of him?"

Audrey wanted to look up at him. She wanted to look into his eyes and see the honesty in his words. But she couldn't. The tears in her own eyes embarrassed her.

"I think the Lord is drawing him," Brent said. "He had questions about how I was able to change. I was telling him my story."

"You believed him?" Audrey asked, incredulously. "He came to you asking questions about God and salvation, saying how badly he wanted to change, and you believed him?"

Brent nodded. "He was serious."

"He wasn't serious," Audrey almost snapped. "He's up to something, and the closer you let him get the sorrier we'll be in the end. You're the one who worked so hard to convince me not to let him back in, and here you're the one doing it."

A couple came out of the diner and Audrey caught their rubbernecked glances in her direction.

"I don't want to talk about this here." She opened her purse and began to dig around for keys as she started toward the parking lot.

Brent followed right on her heels. "Audrey, listen to me."

She turned to face him. "Do you know how many times I've heard him say he's changed, or he's trying to change, or he swears he will change, one of these days?"

"I know. I know, and you're right not to trust him."

"He won't change." To her complete chagrin, the tears began to flow. When she began again, her voice was little more than a whisper. "I've spent years waiting for him to change, hoping he would change. Hoping he would quit drinking. Hoping he would stop pushing me around. Hoping he might feel enough love and respect for me to marry me instead of just sleeping with me, and living in my house, and letting me support him."

Brent looked down.

"Finally, after all these years, I realized that no amount of hoping would change him. No amount of anything would change him. You were the one who helped me realize that."

Brent leaned next to her against the car and took her hand in his. "I was wrong. Besides, isn't that what you used to think about me?"

Yes.

This time she looked down. That's exactly what she'd thought about him once.

"I changed," Brent said.

But that's different, she wanted to say, realizing even as the argument drifted through her mind how childish it sounded. Not to mention untrue. It wasn't any different. Not so many weeks ago she had used the same line of reasoning to give Bobby yet another chance to try and prove himself. She had used it to redeem some portion of the time she'd spent living with him, thinking that if Bobby really could change, then they could get married and perhaps right all the wrongs of their life together. Brent had done it. Why not Bobby? She nearly cringed at the thought.

He raised her hand to his mouth and pressed a kiss to the back of it. "The only difference now is that you've forgiven me for treating you so...unforgivably."

Audrey looked back up at him.

"You have forgiven me, haven't you?"

She softened, smiled and sniffed. "Yes. But you're changing the subject. This isn't about you."

Brent shook his head. "No. It's about you."

How did he do that? How had he managed to take this situation–her walking in to find him shaking hands like friends with Bobby–and turn it around, making it about her? She couldn't decide if she would rather throw herself into his arms and weep, or get into her car and drive off.

"I know how you feel," Brent said.

She clenched her teeth.

"After the way he treated you, he doesn't deserve forgiveness, and to forgive him would mean letting your guard down around him. But—"

"I *have* forgiven him!" Audrey snapped. "Time and time again! It's never made any difference. I've probably forgiven him a hundred times."

"Forgive him once more, Audrey. Even if it still doesn't seem to make a difference to you. Forgive him one more time and be done with it. It doesn't mean you have to be friends with him. It doesn't mean you have to trust him. It doesn't even mean you have to like him."

"Have you?" Audrey asked.

"Have I what?"

"Have you forgiven him for everything he did to me?"

Brent looked down.

"Have you?" Her voice was barely audible.

Brent swallowed. "No. But I will. He's lost, Audrey. He's searching."

"He's lying."

"The Bible says—"

"Turn the other cheek. Forgive seventy times seven. I know what the Bible says about it." Audrey almost spat the words.

Brent backed off. He nodded and looked down.

She immediately regretted her vehemence. She took a deep breath and pinched the bridge of her nose, squeezing her eyes shut against another wash of tears.

"Why don't we go back to my house." His soft, low voice eased the hurt a little. "We can find something to eat there, and we can talk about this in private."

She shook her head and opened her eyes. "There's nothing else to say about it."

He stepped aside when she opened her car door and tossed her purse in the passenger seat.

He caught her hand as she lowered herself into the driver's seat. She felt his thumb brush her knuckles and come to rest on the ring he'd given her. Another batch of tears surfaced. "I'll call you later."

She nodded, turned the key in the ignition, and pulled the door closed.

She caught a glimpse of him in the rearview mirror as she pulled out of the parking lot. He was standing right where she'd left him, rubbing the back of his neck with one hand as he watched her drive away.

Audrey swung her legs over the edge of the bed, burying her face in her hands. She'd tossed and turned for hours last night, replaying the argument she'd had with Brent. First she thought she'd been too stubborn. Brent had been right. He had changed completely. She'd even tried to rationalize letting Bobby have his last chance by using Brent's transformation as evidence that Bobby could change, too. But then in the next moment she'd let outrage wash over her again.

She rubbed her face before she dropped her hands and checked the time on her bedside clock. Five fifty-eight a.m. This morning she didn't know how to feel other than exhausted. And she might say that she hadn't slept a bit last night. But she had, because in her dreams Bobby haunted her.

She'd worn the most beautiful white satin gown, and her hair and makeup had been flawless. A sheer veil floated delicately around her shoulders as she walked, beaming, down the aisle to stand beside Brent in front of the preacher. He had smiled joyfully at her and there had been tears in his eyes when he reached for her hand.

Quietly, reverently, Brent had repeated his vows to her. But when her turn came, the church doors flew open and Bobby burst in. He'd stalked down the aisle toward them. Audrey stood frozen.

He said nothing. But his fingertips bit into the flesh of her arm where he grabbed her just above the elbow. For a long moment he stared at her, his ordinarily handsome features twisted by the anger she'd never known the source of, but which had always been directed at her.

She'd flinched as he jerked her away from Brent

and shoved her back down the aisle toward the church foyer. Audrey tried to stay ahead of him, but he was following behind her too quickly. Every time he'd catch up to her he'd shove her harder, causing her to stumble.

Outside the church doors he ripped the bouquet from her hand and threw it away. Then he examined her disdainfully from head to toe.

"White dress," he said with a sneer, grabbing a handful of her satin skirt and holding it up before her. "Did you ever see anything so ridiculous?"

"Please, Bobby," she pleaded, trying in vain to loosen his grip on the fabric of her dress. "Let me go."

"Now why would I want to do that?" He pulled her to him by the satin gripped in his fist and she heard it tear. "If you didn't want to be with me, baby, you should never have let me slip into your booth that night at the diner. You should have never let me lay down with you and do what you knew all along was wrong."

He tore the veil from her head and tossed it away. "And look at you now, trying to be so good and proper. Acting like you and me never happened. Well, he can't have you, baby. You're mine and you always will be."

Audrey looked back over her shoulder to where Brent still stood in the front of the sanctuary. "Make him let me go, Brent," she called to him.

"Forgive him," Brent answered.

Bobby grabbed another handful of her dress and began to shred it with his bare hands.

"Brent, *please!*"

"Brent, please!" Bobby mimicked her. "You see him standing there don't you. He's not coming out here to help you. He knows he can't have you."

"Brent!"

"Forgive him." Brent's voice echoed back to her, intermingling with her own sobs...

Audrey expelled an exhausted breath and pushed hair out of her face with both hands, the details of the dream already beginning to fade and swirl with real memories of her life with Bobby.

Forgive him once more and be done with it.

Those had been Brent's words to her just last night. She sighed and shook her head. But, no. No matter how many times she forgave him, she would never be done with it. Bobby would really haunt her for the rest of her life. He might not break in on her wedding and stop it from happening, but he would always be there. And now it looked as if he would always stand between her and Brent as well.

❧❧

"He wants me to be his sponsor."

The comment seemed to come from nowhere. They'd spent the last twenty minutes eating in relative silence at Audrey's little dining room table.

It *seemed* to come from nowhere. But for the past three days she'd been able to think of little other than Brent's new alliance with Bobby. And now Brent's admission that Bobby wanted him to become some kind of sponsor, proved the subject weighed just as heavily on his mind.

"His sponsor for what?"

"Remember when I told you he was out of jail and that I had seen him?"

She nodded when he paused for confirmation.

"I saw him at an AA meeting."

"AA. As in Alcoholics Anonymous?"

Brent nodded.

"I didn't know you went to AA."

"It was my first meeting since I've been back here."

"Are you OK?" Guilt descended and she reached across the table to lay a hand on his arm. Was he struggling? Was she the cause? Her mind flashed back to the night of the fire, when they'd stored her parents' belongings at his barn. He had told her then that he'd been tempted to drink a couple of times. But that would have been before he saw Bobby out of jail at an AA meeting.

"I'm fine." Brent laid his fork down on his empty plate. "Everything's fine. It's just hard sometimes. My support group was in College Station, my sponsor..." He gave his head a shake as if he didn't know how to explain what he wanted to say.

"It's been hard on you, being back here." She pushed her plate aside and laid her napkin on the table, unable to meet his eyes, overwhelmed by the conviction that she hadn't provided a lick of support for him. It had always been him supporting her. "There must be reminders everywhere."

She finally glanced up to find him staring at his plate, his jaw set, lips pressed together in a firm line. Then he nodded. "It's been better since my mother left. No cases of beer stashed in the fridge..."

"Oh, Brent." She sighed and took his hand, intertwining her fingers with his. She'd had no idea.

"There's an AA meeting this evening, and I feel like I should go."

She nodded. "Of course."

"And Bobby will probably be there. He's asked me to be his sponsor." Brent watched her closely, as if gauging her response. "And I feel like the Lord is leading me to do it."

"You?"

He nodded.

"Brent..." She took a breath and let it out slowly. She wanted them to sever all ties with Bobby. It had to be that way. Bobby would never leave them alone otherwise. But how could she argue with what he felt like God was leading him to do? "I think AA is a good thing for Bobby. It's real progress. But can't someone else be his sponsor?"

"Who, Audrey?"

She shrugged. "I don't know, someone else. There must be–"

"Do you really think he would have asked me if there was anyone else?" Brent heaved a sigh. "Me?"

He had obviously given this a lot of thought, and he didn't want to do it any more than she wanted him to. That realization gave her a measure of comfort. And he was right. Bobby's entire family were outcasts. No one else would help. Bobby had taken a bold step in asking Brent, which only showed how desperate he truly was to change. But how could he possibly change as long as he was still staying out at his mother's house, where his father would sit for days in a drunken stupor watching television and not caring that Bobby's brother, Tommy, carried on their father's hateful tradition of domestic terrorism.

Then there were the questions that silently troubled her since Brent made it so clear that God was truly working in Bobby's life. Why now? Why not a few years ago? Why not when it could have made such an incredible difference in her life as well? Why had she not been reason enough for him to change? What was wrong with her?

There is a love that can reform any man.

The idea drifted through her soul for the first time in months–since she'd come to believe the changes in Brent.

But it is not your love.

The sound of Brent's chair on the wood floor as he pushed away from the table brought her mind back around. He carried his dishes to the sink then came to stand behind her, resting his hands on her shoulders.

"I told him I'd need to talk to you about it." He gave her shoulders a gentle squeeze. "I'd like to have your support, Audrey. And I'll understand if you can't give it. But I'm gonna help him."

He dropped a kiss on her cheek. "I love you. I'll call you later."

She nodded, closed her eyes and breathed deeply, listening as his heavy, booted footsteps carried him through the dining room, then, muffled by the living room carpet, to the front door, which he closed quietly.

かで

"Carlene!" Audrey restrained herself from squealing her friend's name like a giddy girl. But just barely.

Carlene flashed a brilliant smile and let Jim usher her up the front steps of the church. Audrey couldn't remember ever seeing Carlene at church, or hearing her speak of attending a service anywhere. But here she was, and she glowed.

"Oh, Audrey!" Carlene wrapped arms around her

and squeezed. "I got saved!"

"What?" Audrey gasped and took a step back to study her friend. "When?"

"Yesterday, at Jim's Dad's house in Abilene." Joy radiated from her. "Jim's brothers were there and while they were all watching a football game, I fell asleep in the recliner in his dad's office. Well, a little while later his dad came in and accidentally woke me up, and we had the most wonderful conversation. And then Jim came in and the three of us prayed together..." Carlene's eyes glistened. "I know, it probably sounds sappy, but I feel so good..."

Audrey pulled her into another embrace, her own eyes prickling. Happiness for her friend warred with a sense of failure. She had been Carlene's friend for all these years. She should have had more of an influence. And the fact that she hadn't, suddenly underscored in the most noticeable way how the past ten years or so had been totally wasted.

"Oh!" Carlene jerked out of the hug and thrust her left hand forward. "And look!"

A smile emerged through Audrey's sense of inadequacy at the sight of the beautiful band on Carlene's left ring finger.

"It belonged to Jim's mother." Carlene's voice softened to a near whisper. "She gave it to him a few years ago when she was so sick, before she passed away."

Audrey nodded. That had been a hard time for Jim. Cancer had taken his mother when she was still so young. She cast a glance at Jim who had extended his arm toward Brent for a handshake. Jim looked as mellow as ever, his wide, easy smile infectious as usual.

"I'm so happy for you." Audrey gave Carlene's hand another squeeze as a loud, rumbling engine drowned out her words. Bobby's truck turned into the church parking lot.

In the next instant Brent stood at her side. "He hasn't caused any trouble all week." He spoke softly in her ear. "He's not here to cause any trouble for you today, either. Let's just wait and see what happens."

Audrey bristled. For years she'd been just waiting to see what would happen with Bobby. And too often it ended up being anything but good.

He's lost, Audrey. He's searching.

Brent's words from the evening at the Prickly Pear drifted through her mind. But why did he have to be searching now? And why here? How much longer would the sins of her past follow her before she would be free?

But she knew Brent was right. She could feel it in her soul as well. God was working in Bobby's life in a way He never had before. God was working in *her* life in the same way. The uncertainty of what was to come overwhelmed her so suddenly that she swayed and took hold of Brent's arm to steady her suddenly careening heart.

Bobby hadn't made any trouble for her since he'd been arrested the night of the fire. Except for his deceptively casual greeting to her at the diner the other night, he hadn't spoken a word to her. But he was back.

As Bobby parked his truck and stepped out, Audrey turned and let Brent guide her inside. And though she tried to focus elsewhere as the congregants gathered in the sanctuary and began settling into their places, she remained painfully aware of each time the foyer door opened.

She imagined she could feel his eyes on them as they took their seats, but she didn't dare turn around. Images of her recent dream flashed, of Bobby's expression twisted with fury as he tore her from Brent's side. Of his sneer when he'd called her white dress ridiculous. She closed her eyes, hoping to refocus her mind, but that action only made the images sharper.

The congregation rose to sing, but seemed unusually subdued this morning, almost like everyone there could feel the tension that was beginning to make her head ache. It didn't help that, through the whole service, she imagined she could feel Bobby's stare boring into the back of her neck. She hardly heard a word the preacher said.

During the invitation time at the end of the service Audrey prayed. She tried to remember the passage in the book of Matthew that she'd committed to memory so many years ago, the one that instructed her not to be anxious, not to worry, that God would take care of her.

Lord, please. She breathed steadily, eyes squeezed shut. *Please, Lord. I don't know what else to do. I'm so afraid that everything's going to just fall apart at any moment, and I'll be dragged back down again. Please, God. Just make him go away. I'll do whatever you want me to do. Just please make him go away for good.*

She opened her eyes and took a deep breath. The tension that had been building in her neck and shoulders began to ease as peace saturated her soul

When they rose to leave, Bobby was gone. His abrupt absence reinforced the peace she felt now. But freedom from Bobby Kerr could not possibly come that easily.

16

Was that her phone?

Audrey twisted to reach for her purse and shifted the plastic grocery bag to her other hand. The electronic chirp sounded again and she unzipped her purse and began to dig. It was probably Brent calling to see if she was on her way.

Another chirp, less muffled this time. She was getting closer, but she only had one more ring to get to it before her voice mail picked up. Dadgummit! She needed a new purse. A better system. She shoved her wallet out of the way, plunging into the dark depths of the handbag, her hand connecting with the phone as the fourth ring sounded. The strap fell off her shoulder as she pulled the phone free, but she caught it before it hit the ground.

"Hello?"

Too late. One missed call.

She pulled the purse back into place and kept her eyes on the little screen, waiting for the message as she continued on through the store exit.

Of course, now she needed her keys.

Back into the depths she went, walking as she dug, until she slammed right into someone in her path.

"Oh!" The impact shook the purse off her shoulder again, and she grabbed for it as a strong pair of arms — familiar arms — reached out to steady her. The sensation of Bobby's arms, even in such an innocent context, stunned her to stillness. And even after she realized she should extract herself from his hold by the quickest means possible, another part of her stood, almost hypnotized, by the difference she saw in his expression, by the sudden impression that something about him really had changed this time.

"You OK?"

She shook the feeling off. Dismissed it as stupid. "Um...yeah. Excuse me."

He looked as if he wanted to say something but remained silent as he stepped aside and let her pass.

"Audrey?"

She stopped just short of the parking lot and stood for a long moment, debating. If she didn't turn around...if she just continued on to her car, the message would be clear. But she couldn't disregard the shared history. As much as she wanted to, she couldn't just pretend that she had never known him, that he was just a stranger. She turned around.

"Can I talk to you?"

"You're talking to me, Bobby."

"Maybe a little more privately?" He glanced around them.

"No." She turned back around and took a step toward the parking lot.

"Audrey, please." His guileless tone softened her heart slightly and she stopped again. "I need to talk to you."

She sighed heavily and turned to face him again. "No. You don't need to talk to me. There's nothing to say."

"But if I could just–"

"No, Bobby. It's not a good idea." She turned

away from him and dug frantically in her purse for keys as she hurried to her car. A quick glance back when she got there revealed that he hadn't followed her. He still stood, right where she left him on the sidewalk, watching her. His shoulders sagged and he heaved a very heavy sigh, looking like he might just cry.

Something inside told her to call out to him as he turned to enter the store. Suddenly, from out of nowhere, her heart started to pound. Tears stung her eyes as she recognized God's prompting, and the very Voice within seemed to speak under His authority.

Audrey gritted her teeth hard as Bobby disappeared through the door.

Go after him.

She heard the command in her mind.

Let him ask forgiveness, then give it to him. It's what he needs.

Her hands trembled and she gritted her teeth even harder. Forgiveness usually came so easily. She had forgiven Bobby countless times, and he hadn't just hurt her feelings once or twice. He had abused her. He'd left bruises and even a few permanent scars. He had degraded and humiliated her. He caused her to lose their child. He didn't deserve her forgiveness.

This grudge she felt justified in holding on to. She *needed* to hold on to it. She was afraid to let it go. Everything she wanted and seemed to have within her grasp—Brent, marriage, a home, a family—depended on her holding this grudge forever.

Go after him. Forgive him. It's what he needs.

Audrey shook her head and stood her ground. "What about what I need?"

⤜⤛

At church on Sunday morning Brent greeted Audrey with a soft kiss on the cheek.

Bobby was already seated in what was becoming his usual spot on the very back row. She walked past him, carefully avoiding any kind of eye contact, though Brent gave him a cordial nod. Brent's hand at her back provided little solace as he guided her into the pew beside her parents. And when the congregation began to sing during the praise and worship time, she couldn't. Heaviness pressed down like a lead vest, and it was all she could do to remain standing. Her hands trembled and her ears began to ring. But above the ringing, or maybe within it, she thought she heard her name whispered.

She squeezed eyes shut and gripped the back of the pew, holding on until the songs ended and she could sit down. Brent slid an arm around her shoulders and settled down to listen to the preacher as if nothing was different. As if he had no sense that something strange was happening.

A discreet glance told her everything seemed normal. Nothing odd or out of place. People settled down, opened their Bibles, and turned their attention to the pastor as he began his opening remarks. But she hardly heard a word he said. How could she, absorbed in this unrest. Ten minutes must have passed while she tried unsuccessfully to tamp down this agitation.

Lord? Are you here? Are you listening? What's wrong with me? Do you see what I'm going through?

Of course He did. It was silly to think otherwise.

Pray for Bobby.

Audrey breathed deeply and felt the sting of tears.

Would the man never go away? Would she never be free?

Lord, please. I'll do whatever you ask.

Brent glanced at her and squeezed her shoulders comfortingly.

But will you do whatever I ask, even if Bobby never goes away?

She reached up with one hand and pinched the bridge of her nose as a familiar ache rose up in her throat. Would she? She kind of wanted some details first.

Return to me, Audrey.

But I have.

Return to me completely. With your whole heart, withholding nothing.

Haven't I?

"Therefore, if anyone is in Christ, he is a new creation; the old has gone, the new has come!"

Audrey blinked at the sensation that the words had just been shouted at her. But she couldn't tell from where. The pulpit? Her own imagination? She glanced up to find that the preacher had stopped preaching and now stood silently. The entire congregation seemed to be holding its breath. What was going on? What had she missed? Brent pulled his arm from her shoulders and leaned forward, his Adam's apple drifting up, then down again as he swallowed.

All the little hairs on her neck and arms prickled at the sudden electricity in the air. She sucked in her breath and held it, waiting for the next words from the preacher. A charge ran through the building, as if everyone there was waiting expectantly for the same thing. But he didn't speak. He stepped down off the platform instead and raised an arm toward the back.

Brent clasped his hands and pressed them to his forehead, praying. As if he knew exactly what was going on. Audrey glanced behind her.

Bobby stood in the middle of the aisle, looking stunned.

"Come on," the preacher said.

Bobby lurched forward and came quickly up the aisle. Not running. Holding himself back. Yet seeming like he couldn't get there fast enough.

He's lost, Audrey. He's searching. Brent's words came to her again.

She cast a glance to the front of the sanctuary where the pastor now stood with his hands on Bobby's shoulders. Their heads were so close together they nearly touched as they spoke.

Both men closed their eyes and bowed their heads as the pastor prayed over Bobby, but she couldn't make out the words. Brent prayed in a whisper beside her, tears wetting his cheeks.

"Oh, God!" Bobby's cry from the front drew her attention back to him. He staggered, as if under some weight. Then he dropped to his knees. "God, forgive me!"

He buried his face in his hands and hung his head so low that she couldn't see him beyond the people sitting in front of her. The music director rose and directed the congregation to do the same. The pianist began playing a hymn as the words were projected onto the screen behind the pulpit. The congregation began to sing.

Blessed assurance, Jesus is mine.

Brent left her side and headed down front.

Oh what a foretaste of glory divine.

He must have nearly prostrated himself beside

Bobby and the pastor because she couldn't see him either, even when she went up on her tiptoes.

Heir of salvation, purchase of God,

Men's voices floated up above the music. She could hear them distinctly, even though the words were obscured.

Born of his Spirit, washed in His blood.

Not that the words mattered.

This is my story, this is my song; praising my Savior all the day long.

This is my story, this is my song; praising my Savior all the day long.

Bobby's heart had changed. In that very moment the old was gone and the new had come, and the words hardly mattered at all. Audrey squeezed her eyes shut, sending a cascade of tears down her cheeks. She swayed as her knees threatened to buckle, and an arm came gently around her waist–her mother's arm–guiding her down onto the pew, where she remained with her eyes shut tightly until the congregation made it through a few more verses, then stilled.

When she opened her eyes, Bobby stood before them all, looking brand new. There could be no disputing his conversion. It resonated in her heart, even though her mind rebelled and refused to believe it had happened. She shook her head.

Six months. That's all she would give him before he slipped right back into his old way of living. Six months at the most.

"Most of us know Bobby Kerr." The pastor began. "He comes to us this morning making his profession of faith. Please come and welcome him into our family."

Usually when someone professed their faith, a chorus of "amen's" rang throughout the sanctuary. But this morning, it seemed, it wasn't only Audrey who remained skeptical. Stunned silence filled the sanctuary.

The preacher cleared his throat and motioned for Brent to come and stand beside Bobby.

Brent beamed as he stood and shook Bobby's hand. And that's all it took.

The whole congregation came back to life and a line formed immediately. And all it took was the endorsement of Brent Thomason, a man who, ten years ago, had been considered little better than Bobby.

At least Audrey's parents hadn't joined the line, and there were a few others who turned and made their way from the building without joining in. But even so, it seemed only a few didn't want to shake the hand that had struck her so many times.

Audrey gathered her purse and Bible and turned to leave.

"We should wait for Brent," her mother said gently.

"You go ahead." The words came out as a whisper.

Her dad's arm came around her shoulders and he gave her a comforting squeeze as they walked toward the foyer together. Outside in the parking lot Audrey turned to find that her mother followed them after all, and now Brent had torn himself away from his new friend to join them.

"Audrey, wait."

But she didn't wait. She didn't even acknowledge him. She couldn't without totally melting down right here on the pavement. What just happened? And how was she supposed to respond? Was she really supposed to just forget her past with Bobby, all the unspeakable ways he treated her? Had the cosmic slate been wiped clean? Really? Where was the justice? She turned and pulled her car door open. Brent snagged her wrist and turned her to face him, refusing to be ignored.

Something in her snapped at the touch. "Are *you* gonna hit me now, too? What's it gonna be, your fist or the back of your hand? Maybe you should run inside real quick and ask the man who knows all my most sensitive spots since y'all are such good friends now."

Brent dropped her arm.

"Audrey, I would never..."

Audrey looked down. She knew he would never strike her. Her words had been intended to shock and hurt him, and she'd obviously hit her mark. She turned and put her things in the car, then pressed her fingertips to her eyes for a long moment hoping to clear the turmoil enough to think more clearly and sort through all the emotions which stood now in direct opposition to the miraculous regeneration that had just occurred inside.

When she tried to speak again, all she could do was whisper. "You're supposed to be on my side."

"I'm always on your side." Brent glanced up at Lyndon, who refused to go away. "But this isn't about sides. What happened here today isn't about you or me, or even Bobby. It's about God's mercy and grace."

She folded arms across her chest and looked back toward the church as people continued to file out.

"I was where he is now about six years ago." Brent swallowed and cleared his throat. "And, thank God, there was someone willing to help me through it."

"That's just fine." She found a remnant of anger to cling to. "But do you know where I was about six years ago? I was trying my best to make it back to work with bruised ribs and black eyes so that I could pay my rent. So that he would have a place to live. So that he would have a couch to sit on and a television to watch while he got drunk and mad. So that he...so that..."

Her voice trailed off as she looked up at him, her eyes brimming. His expression, urgent in its honesty, revealed an understanding of her struggle. He gently pressed the palm of his hand to her cheek.

"I'm on your side. Trust me, Audrey. If I'm completely wrong about this, if this is all a lie, I'll never let Bobby lay another hand on you. I won't even let him say another word to you."

Brent brushed a tear off her cheek with his thumb.

"But I have to believe this is real for him." He paused, and Audrey watched as he choked up. When he continued his voice was rough and unsteady. "I have to believe this is as real for him as it was for me."

He unfolded her arms by taking both her hands in his.

"But please, Audrey, don't quit on us because of this. I'm not going to demand that you forgive him, though I still think you should. But please, tell me this isn't going to break us up."

Audrey looked down at strong hands as they held hers. As she left the church building she'd entertained the first thought of giving his ring back and calling the engagement off. When she turned to find him following her she'd thought of ripping it from her finger and throwing it back at him right then and there, and chalking the whole mess up to her continued bad judgment.

But she loved Brent, and the still small Voice in her heart, the one she'd been fighting so hard against, compelled her to wait, and not do anything rash.

She gave his hands a squeeze and shook her head. "I don't know, Brent," she said. "I just need to think about all this."

Brent swallowed hard and looked down. Then he nodded. "I love you," he said, his voice hoarse. "Think about that."

17

"So, is it hard to stand here and look at it?" Audrey came to stand beside her mother, who surveyed the freshly cleared foundation where her home once stood.

"I guess." Her mom shrugged. "I'll miss the house. But we'll build another. I think I'll really miss the things that we weren't able to save inside it."

In a few days it would be October. The worst of the summer heat was over for Blithe Settlement, at least for the next several months, after which the sun would scorch the earth again. But this morning, Audrey needed a sweater for the first time since April. And for now, the brisk temperature and morning breeze were a welcome change. Audrey breathed deeply and relished the first nip of autumn on her nose and cheeks.

"I suppose none of it really belonged to us anyway," her mother continued. "'The Lord giveth, and the Lord taketh away.'"

Audrey glanced sideways at her mother with a smirk.

"I know," her mom said. "It's trite. But it's true. Look what I have. I have a husband who has loved me for more than thirty years, and we have a home together even if we don't have a house right now. I have a beautiful daughter who has loved me for nearly thirty years, who will soon be married and having my grandchildren."

"Mom—"

"I know." Paula raised a hand. "You and Brent have hit a little rough patch. It'll be the first of many. But you'll work it out. Anyway, my point is this: if God never gives me another thing in this life, He has blessed me so richly that I can't even begin to thank Him."

Her gratitude was contagious. Audrey felt it, too. She had her parents, and her father was recovering well from his depression. She had Brent, who loved her at last. And while she could never right the wrongs of her past, she at least had the chance to live better from now on. *Thank you, Lord, for that chance.* The feeling washed over her soul like she'd wanted to let the rain wash over her body that night at the Prickly Pear; the night Brent had proposed. Audrey took hold of her mother's hand and gave it a squeeze.

"Audrey," her mom began, "I've always tried to let you live your own life without butting in too much. Even when I thought you needed more than a good talking to, like when you let Bobby move in with you. I've tried not to push you too hard. I should have been a little nosier at times. Maybe I should have been a little more insistent that you do some things differently. I'll always think, on some level, that what you suffered at the hands of that man was my fault."

"Mom, no—"

"I think I like Bobby even less than you do, honey. To watch somebody treat my child in such a way–my baby..." Her voice broke and her face contorted with sudden emotion. "And to just have to stand by and watch, and be powerless to stop it..." She pressed her lips together and took a deep breath, struggling to regain control. "But him coming to know Christ. That's a good thing. And if he is really trying to quit drinking and change, if he's really trying this time, that's a good thing, too.

"But even if he's lying, or if he's not lying and he just fails, that part of your life is over now. Regardless of what he decides to do with the rest of his life, that part is over for you. Don't let it haunt you forever. Don't let it make you angry and bitter. Don't let it turn you from the man who loves you." Her mom stroked Audrey's hair, pushing a lock behind one ear, like she had so many times when Audrey had been a girl. "Let it go, honey."

An unexpected sob shook her. Then another came, and another, and she let them keep coming. It felt like a tidal wave, all this sadness and joy, anger and fear, regret and repentance. But after the wave had crashed, drenching her soul, then returning to its source; it left peace in its wake.

She wanted to fall to her knees and weep for all the trials she'd put herself through, as well as for the grace and mercy that God still extended despite all the years she'd gone her own way. But her mother pulled her into a tight embrace and held her for what seemed like an eternity.

"I'm sorry," she whispered through repentant tears. "God, please forgive me."

"Shh." Her mother stroked her hair.

The sound of tires on gravel reinstated her sense of time and place, and the tears abated.

"Now," Paula pulled free from Audrey's clinging embrace and smiled, her own eyes brimming. "Go on over there and work it out."

Brent had stepped from his truck and stood, leaning against it, watching them.

Audrey nodded and kissed her mother's cheek. "I love you, Mom."

Brent stood straight as she approached. The uncertain look on his face pierced like a knife to the heart, and the knowledge that she'd put it there only served to twist that knife. For her, there was no doubt how she and Brent would end up.

And Bobby...well, Bobby had the right to live his life, and go to church, and get saved. And Brent had the right to walk him through it. That Brent *would* do that only underscored the fact that he was exactly the kind of man who would always try his best to do the right thing. And wasn't that what she'd always wanted?

When she reached him, she clutched a handful of his denim jacket and kissed him without preamble. He tensed, in surprise no doubt, but only for a second or two before his arms slid around and he took over, wrapping her in his warmth.

"Hey!" Her dad's voice, coming from the direction of the small stockyard, pierced their little bubble. "Cut that out and get to work!"

A slow smile emerged on Brent's face, mirroring hers.

"April tenth." Audrey straightened his jacket as best she could from within the circle of his arms.

His brow furrowed. "What?"

"It's a Saturday. Check your calendar. I've already checked on the church, and it's available. The bluebonnets should be out, so we could get some pictures made in that field just west of there. Carlene has already agreed to be my maid of honor, or would that be matron of honor? You should probably decide who your best man is gonna be." The slightly bewildered expression on his face made her pause. "What?"

He shook his head and grinned. "Nothing."

ॐ

The guineas that Jim brought from his brother's place, made more noise than anything Audrey ever heard. But she hadn't had to sweep crickets off the front porch, so she hadn't complained. This morning they screeched and clucked as they scurried out of her way. She could have sworn he'd only brought three or four, but it seemed like every few days one more appeared, and they made every bit as much racket as twenty.

"Sorry I'm late," Audrey called as she threw her purse in her desk drawer and turned on the computer.

No one started the coffee, so she put a fresh filter into the coffee maker and started measuring the usual amount. She turned, coffee pot in hand, to head down the hall for some water, just in time to witness Jim trying to sneak from Carlene's office.

He was straightening his glasses when he realized he'd been caught. Traces of suspiciously red lipstick still lingered, smudged around his mouth.

"Um, you're late."

"I'm surprised you noticed." Audrey pointed to the corner of her mouth.

Jim pulled a handkerchief from his pocket and began wiping his own. He examined the new stains on the white cloth, then folded it with a telling smile, put it back, and continued down the hall.

Carlene didn't emerge until Audrey finished preparing the coffee and turning on the pot. Her freshly applied lipstick was flawless.

Audrey sat behind her desk, shot her friend a grin, and shook her head.

"What?" Carlene asked, all innocence.

"You're so easy."

A slow smile spread across Carlene's face, and she sat on the corner of Audrey's desk, crossing one leg over the other as elegantly as she could considering the bump of her belly clearly showed now. The bell on the front door jingled, and Bobby walked in.

"Well, well. Look who's here. Should I just go ahead and call the police now?" Carlene kept her voice low, but not so low that Bobby didn't hear her warning.

Audrey shook her head. "No. It'll be fine."

For an awkward moment they all just stood and looked at each other. Bobby relented, took his old, worn baseball cap off, and looked down first.

"Could I speak to you in private, Audrey?"

Audrey nodded and glanced at Carlene who was clearly reluctant to leave the room. Finally, however, she hopped off Audrey's desk.

"OK. I'll just be in my office. With the door open. You call me if you need anything."

Bobby watched as Carlene left the room with deliberate slowness. After she'd gone, he looked down at his boots and swallowed hard. He took a few steps toward her desk.

"I don't know where to start," he said finally. "I know you don't want to hear anything I have to say, but I had to take a chance coming here today."

Audrey folded her arms and leaned back in the

chair.

"I've been going to AA meetings. For about a month now. I haven't had a drink in all that time. Not one."

He smiled, and her heart lurched. For an instant she saw the precious child he must have once been, an impression she'd only ever had of him when the hard lines of his face had been completely relaxed in sleep. But she had seen it then, just as she saw it now. There *was* a good man inside him. *Lord, help him.*

"I really am tryin' this time. I know you've heard that from me a hundred times, and I don't blame you for not believing me. I'm not trying to sneak my way back into your life. I know you're with Brent now. I know you're gonna marry him. He's made it pretty clear to me that he's your man now."

Bobby paused and swallowed, then he cleared his throat. "I'm glad for you, baby. I am. I know how much he means to you, and I'm not here to try and ruin that."

"What are you here for, Bobby?" Her quiet question seemed to make him even more unsure. He clutched his cap in both hands and took a deep breath.

"I...I need to ask your forgiveness. You most of all, Audrey. For the way I treated you, the things I did...I truly never wanted to, and I want you to know it wasn't your fault. You weren't what made me so angry all the time. You were the one good thing I had. I didn't deserve you then, and I don't deserve you now. But I want you to know how sorry I am. Please don't cry, baby. I'm sorry."

Audrey hadn't even realized the tears had pooled in her eyes. But when she blinked, they spilled over.

Bobby had tears in his eyes, too. But this time,

maybe for the first time, he tried hard to hold them back. He looked down and made an effort to compose himself. "Please forgive me," he said, wringing his cap in his hands, his voice little more than a whisper.

This time Audrey followed the prompting when it hit her. She rose from her chair and came around her desk. For a split second Bobby looked as if he might turn and run. He actually took a step backward as she approached. *That* was ironic. But he relaxed when she clasped his hands in hers, ball cap and all.

"I forgive you, Bobby."

A tear did roll down his cheek then. He swallowed and looked down again as he nodded. "Thank you."

He smiled in a way she'd never seen before. He looked relieved, and he looked happy, even joyful.

Her part was done. She let go of his hands and backed up a step. But he reached out and pulled her to him, wrapping his arms tightly around her. Panic flared and her hands went up reflexively to push him away. But he only stood there holding on.

"I'm getting baptized on Sunday," he said hoarsely. "It'd sure mean a lot to me if you were there. Will you come?"

Audrey nodded.

"You will?"

"I'll be there."

He let out a deep breath, as if he'd been holding it for years. Although she couldn't see his face, locked in his embrace as she was, she could almost feel him smile.

"You are so precious to me, Audrey," he whispered against her hair. "You'll never know how much you've meant to me."

Epilogue

"Look, look, look, Jim!" Carlene held out her arms to her daughter, who stood on shaky legs and grinned hugely, displaying four little teeth. "She's gonna do it! Come on, Abby! Come here to Mama!"

Audrey stopped slicing into the chocolate pie on the counter and held her breath, waiting expectantly. Beside her, Brent set a stack of dessert plates down and also turned to watch.

Abby bounced in place a few times, as if testing her knees. Then with another grin she lifted one foot and put it down again, stopping to catch her balance. Then she did the same thing with the other foot.

"That's it, Abby, come on!" Carlene encouraged her.

It took about four wobbly steps for Abby to make it to her mother's arms, at which point she was swept up and covered with kisses as all the grownups burst into cheers and applause.

Abby answered with a high pitched squeal.

"That calls for a piece of pie." Audrey laughed and turned back to her task, slicing and serving a piece for each of them.

Carlene and Jim were great parents. And Abby was the light of their life and a joy to see. Brent especially enjoyed watching the baby, who would officially be a toddler any minute now. Maybe soon the

Lord would bless them with a baby of their own.

Soon, Lord. Please.

She handed Brent two plates laden with pie and forks, and he turned to pass them on to Jim and Carlene. Audrey sighed quietly. She had hoped to be pregnant in time to tell him on their first anniversary. A smile touched her lips at the reaction he would have had. But their anniversary would be here in three days time, and no pregnancy. Maybe next year.

A light knock sounded on the kitchen door. Audrey licked a smudge of meringue off her thumb and went to answer it, smiling to find Bobby on the back stoop. She swung the door open and he stepped inside.

Bobby had been true to everything that had happened in his life. He'd been sober for over a year and a half, a faithful attendee of AA by his own admission, and an even more faithful attendee at church. If she hadn't witnessed it first hand, Audrey would never really believe such a change was even possible. But, praise God, it was.

"Well, it's getting late." Carlene's smile vanished and she pushed her chair back away from the kitchen table, clutching Abby tightly, and reaching for her diaper bag.

Bobby looked down. "It's OK, Carlene, y'all don't have to leave. I'm not staying."

Carlene still had not forgiven Bobby. She had grudgingly admitted that his conversion had *probably* been sincere. But she watched and waited expectantly for him to fall back into his old patterns of living.

Audrey closed the door quietly. "You're welcome to stay, Bobby. You want some pie?"

Brent offered his hand and Bobby shook it.

"Um...no...thanks."

Jim stayed neutrally where he was.

Bobby's gaze slid back to Audrey, and she noticed for the first time the sad longing that Carlene swore she always saw when he looked at her.

"I just came to say good-bye."

"Good-bye?" Brent furrowed his brow. "You going somewhere?"

Bobby nodded and returned his attention to Brent. "Yeah. It's time I moved on. I have a cousin who has a chain of feed stores out in West Texas. He's opening a new one in Lubbock. He's gonna let me manage it for him. He's a good Christian guy. And I'll get better pay, better hours, benefits..." His voice trailed off and he nodded as his attention slid back to Audrey. "It'll be a good move for me. A chance to really start over. Everyone knows me here and hardly anybody really thinks I've changed for good."

Carlene looked down at her shoes.

"Bobby—" Brent took a step toward him, the lines of his face furrowed in concern.

But Bobby held up a hand. "I'm not looking for a geographical cure. Just a fresh start. I could go to AA every night of the week in Lubbock. And I will if I have to."

It felt like a blow to the chest. He was leaving. After all that happened.

Her mind flashed back to a time when she'd sat in church, not believing that the Lord was working a change in his life. She had promised to do anything God required, if He would just make Bobby go away for good. Those might have even been her very words. And now it was coming to pass.

God had required that she forgive Bobby, and she

had. Truly and completely. And now he was leaving. For good. And she wasn't sure how she felt about it. Tears pricked her eyes.

"Well, I'm happy for you, Bobby." She closed the gap between them of her own accord, and reached out to pat his arm. "I know you'll do fine."

Bobby leaned toward her and placed a quick kiss on her cheek.

"You take care of yourself," she whispered hoarsely. "Let us hear from you, OK?"

Bobby nodded and swallowed hard.

Brent extended his hand and Bobby shook it again. "You leaving tonight?"

"Tomorrow morning. First thing."

Brent nodded. "Let us know when you get there and get settled. Let us know you're OK."

Bobby took a deep breath and swallowed hard. "I will. Thanks for everything." With a final nod Bobby turned and left.

Silence engulfed them except for the rumble of his diesel engine as he drove away. Instinctively Audrey reached for Brent and he was there, pulling her into a warm embrace, then cupping her face tenderly, brushing away her tears.

"Maybe we should go." Carlene's quiet assertion broke the silence.

Audrey sniffed. "No." Then she turned and picked up the other two servings of pie and carried them to the table. "Come sit down and eat your pie. And be sure and give plenty to Abby. If you won't, I will."

Carlene smiled at her and sat down. "You just want to get her all sugared up before bedtime, don't you?"

"I just like to help keep things interesting for you."

"Just you wait." Carlene took a bite of her pie. "Your turn's comin'."

Audrey felt her smile return and glanced at Brent. *Soon, Lord. Please.*

Coming June 2011

Moving On
Blythe Settlement #3

Meagan Layne longs for a traditional life as a wife and mother. Love, marriage to an honorable man, a stable home life for her son, more children; it shouldn't be too much to ask. So how did she end up divorced from a man who left her in debt, with a small son to support on a budget that barely meets at the ends?

Bobby Kerr despises his past and wants to build on the new start he made when he left his small hometown for Lubbock. He's a new man in Christ, but he can't forget the violent man he was. He won't subject another woman to the perils of life with him.

But Meagan stirs Bobby's heart in a dangerous way, making him hope that love could be possible for him after all. If she's willing to risk it.